VOICES
FROM THE SKY

VOICES
FROM THE SKY

Jan S. Doward

Pacific Press Publishing Association
Boise, Idaho
Montemorelos, Nuevo Leon, Mexico
Oshawa, Ontario, Canada

Designed by Tim Larson
Cover photo by Gregory Heisler from The Image Bank

Copyright © 1985 by
Pacific Press Publishing Association
Printed in United States of America
All Rights Reserved

Library of Congress Cataloging in Publication Data

Doward, Jan S.
    Voices from the sky.

    Includes bibliographies.
    1. Bible. N.T. Revelation XIV, 6-12—Criticism, in-
terpretation, etc. 2. Seventh-Day Adventists—Doctrines. 3. Doward, Jan S. I. Title.
BS2825.2.D68   1985   230′.6732   84-26427

ISBN 0-8163-0598-6

85 86 87 88 89 • 6 5 4 3 2 1

Contents

Misplaced Dynamite

During the latter part of World War II, the troopship *Admiral W. L. Capps* slipped her Seattle moorings and headed for the Pacific theater of war. Fighting was fierce as the Japanese desperately struggled for their very existence. I was one of the 5,000 GIs crammed aboard this unescorted ship bound for the combat zone. Tensions increased with each passing day. Somewhere up ahead in that vast, impatient wilderness, which is the Pacific Ocean, I had a rendezvous with God.

It happened one evening just about the time orders came over the loudspeakers for all troops to go below. While slowly making my way across the deck, I saw the great Southern Cross twinkling off the port side. It seemed to symbolize a tremendous longing in my life. Already at age 19 I had been totally immersed in the church affairs of a large, liberal Protestant denomination. From childhood I certainly was church oriented. But although I professed to be a Christian, I did not know Christ. And that was frightfully disturbing to me. Suddenly all the thoughts and feelings that had been building up within me swirled into a vortex of need. I was never one to display emotions in public, but right then and there I dropped to my knees on that steel deck and poured out the deepest longings of my heart to know Him. Something like an electric shock seemed to pass clear through me. When I arose the most profound sense of peace settled over me. I was a new person. And I realized that I had finally found the beginning of a relationship with the same Jesus whose own cross was not a starry one against the sky but anchored deep in the rocky ground of Golgotha.

Shortly after this I met another GI whose cheerful attitude and smiles attracted me. Floyd Cromwell stood tall among the men. His one-time crewcut had grown half out so that his blond hair flopped back and forth like some signal flag. He carried his Bible wherever he went, and since he never seemed to buckle his combat boots, the tinkling of those buckles always announced his presence wherever he walked. Something about this big, friendly ex-prizefighter with the broken nose drew me to him. I was desperately hungry right then to know more about the Bible, and I couldn't think of anyone I would rather have help me than Floyd.

"My mother gave me a small pocket New Testament before I shipped out, but I've never read much of it. Would you mind studying the Bible with me?" I asked.

He smiled. "Sure. When shall we start?"

The only possible place for any semblance of privacy was down on the mess deck. Even though it was extremely hot below, that's where we went to study. Both the starboard and port doors were flung wide open to capture as much ventilation as possible, but it was precious little. Down there the cooks, stripped to the waist, their bodies glistening with perspiration from the saunalike heat, moved in slow motion. It was here, though, that the Word of God suddenly came alive for me for the first time. Day after day as the ship zig-zagged its way, Floyd and I would go below to study. Placing our Bibles on one of the chest-high mess tables, we would explore the Scriptures together. He was an excellent teacher, never moving ahead until I understood clearly.

One day while covering a verse-by-verse study of Revelation, Floyd asked, "Would you like to see where Seventh-day Adventists are in prophecy?"

I was stunned. Floyd had never discussed any particular church affiliation with me before, and the name Seventh-day Adventist meant nothing to me. I had heard it used a few times before, but that was all. Their teachings and practice were totally foreign to me. I was skeptical.

"Aw, you can't show me from the Bible!" I exclaimed.

"Come back tomorrow, and I'll show you."

Floyd was a master psychologist. I wanted him to tell me right then and there, but he refused on the grounds that we had studied enough for that day. I could hardly wait. The next day I bounded down to the mess deck to hear his proof. And for the first time in my life I read the passage in Revelation 12:17:

"And the dragon was wroth with the woman, and went to make war with the remnant of her seed, which keep the commandments of God, and have the testimony of Jesus Christ."

Then in his own inimitable way Floyd led me through a sweeping history of God's people and Satan's attack on them down through the ages. Before me opened the truth about those who had remained loyal to the Lord by representing His character through His law and held firmly to the testimony of Jesus Christ, which, according to Revelation 19:10, is the "spirit of prophecy." For the first time I understood how God would have a people on earth when Jesus returns who would uphold the same truths from that long line of faithful believers.

Shortly after landing on Okinawa I was determined to take my stand with the remnant church. No Adventist chaplain was available, and the Baptist chaplain assigned to our outfit refused to baptize me because I wanted to become a Seventh-day Adventist. Floyd borrowed a jeep and drove clear to the south end of the island to where the army was still mopping up the last of the Japanese resistance and found a major who outranked our chaplain. The word came back: "Baptize this man even if he wants to become a Buddhist! You are here to serve the men!"

So on Sunday, July 15, 1945, I was baptized by a Baptist chaplain at Ishikawa Beach. He consented to perform the rite on condition that I take out membership in his church and later transfer. Mine was probably the briefest membership his church ever had!

The subsequent years offered opportunities for further study at college and graduate school, but none could replace nor do much to amplify the profound Bible study that day aboard ship so many years ago when Floyd opened Revelation 12:17 to my understanding.

Adventists early laid claim to this text as evidence that it set forth the earmarks of the true remnant people of God. The strength of keeping the commandments and having the spirit of prophecy in the writings of Ellen White were sufficient evidence.

But as the nineteenth century gave way to the twentieth and the decades have continued to slip away, something seems to have happened to the remnant itself. Some are saying that the motivating drive that sparked the fire of the founding fathers to make such a claim seemingly has all but died out. In its place has come a whole new shift of emphasis.

The story is told of an English farmer who dug a well on his property. He struck water and had it tested by the local health authorities. The water was discovered to possess excellent medicinal properties. Word spread, and soon people were coming with their jugs and jars to obtain his "miracle" water. It wasn't long before the circle widened, and more people heard the good news. Finally the farmer had to provide some accommodations for those traveling long distances. In time an entire village grew up on that end of his farm. The news kept spreading. More and more people came, until finally that small village with a few places of lodging and shops grew into a large city engulfing all the surrounding farmland. Today it is a thriving metropolis with great factories belching smoke and teeming millions busily engaged in making a livelihood.

An American tourist visited the place a few years ago and, fascinated by the historical account, went to the city hall for information.

"I've heard so much about this place," he said. "Just

where is the well located that started this great city?"

The clerk looked up sheepishly. "That is a frightfully embarrassing question," he answered, "but the fact is we can't find the well." These people had lost the source of their beginnings!

In the process of preparing for Christ's soon coming and heaven, Seventh-day Adventists have built churches and schools, hospitals, publishing houses, and food factories. Humming industries have kept up a cash flow, and there is an abundance of machinery to keep up the constant image of growth and prosperity. We have made a reasonable showing financially, materially, and in membership growth, BUT WE ARE STILL HERE! Could it be that we need to go back to the source of our beginnings and rediscover the truths that established the remnant in the first place?

Out of the night of delusion and darkness at the end of the papal supremacy, God called out a people from every nation and tongue to demonstrate once and for all time the truth about Himself. The remnant church, prophetically arising on time, was designed by God to enhance the quality of life here and now and to prepare a people to stand in the great day of Christ's return.

Undoubtedly the greatest wealth of spiritual truths and the most soul-jarring warnings ever entrusted to man have been committed to the Seventh-day Adventists to be shared with the world.[1]

And this has aroused the enemy, alias the great dragon, the old serpent, the devil, or Satan. And so the final phase of the long-standing struggle began in earnest. He is angry with the remnant!

Satan knows that he has but a short time. It is now or never with him. Since sin is of such a self-destructive nature, the enemy has unleashed forces of evil that are beyond his own ability totally to control or to halt. He is caught in the meshes of his own machinations.

Satan also has to hurry, because God is proving through at least a few of His people that the enemy is a liar. There really are some who would rather die than knowingly commit a wrong act—who would go to the wall for their faith! This fact makes the enemy extremely nervous.

Over nineteen centuries have elapsed since Christ silenced the devil's charges that God is not sacrificial. The wrath of the enemy cannot now be directed toward Christ personally, so he puts forth every effort to reach His representatives. The battle is very real. And how has this warfare gone—this battle with the remnant church? Heaven's warning to us as a people is clear. Listen:

"I have been shown that the spirit of the world is fast leavening the church. You are following the same path as did ancient Israel. There is the same falling away from your high calling as God's peculiar people."[2]

"Satan's snares are laid for us as verily as they were laid for the children of Israel just prior to their entrance into the land of Canaan. We are repeating the history of that people. Lightness, vanity, love of ease and pleasure, selfishness, and impurity are increasing among us."[3]

"The church has turned back from following Christ her Leader and is steadily retreating toward Egypt."[4]

As we take a close look at ourselves, we are forced to face some sobering conclusions. Every indication from divinely-inspired sources points to the painful fact that the second coming is long overdue. Jesus longs to have His professed people turn from their gods of pride and passion. Unconsciously we have followed a modernized, sophisticated form of Baal worship. We are here because we want to be—because we have accepted a kind of idolatry that satisfies us.

To be sure, many Adventists have not bowed the knee to the god of some self-seeking Baal. They can stand the winds of strife, because their roots go deep into the love of God. These are the kind of people who will go to the wall for their faith no matter where they live.

But far too many of us have grown lax in our worship of the true God and have unconsciously exchanged the Saviour for some system—some customized, self-aggrandizing god that keeps us comfortable and secure.

In a sense we are all part of this pattern. None of us have any cause to feel smug or spiritually complacent. All of us constitute part of the whole. Like Daniel, who placed himself right alongside his confused, rebellious people, we are all at fault. "We have sinned," he prayed, "and have committed iniquity, and have done wickedly." Daniel 9:5. And we have—we have before us the sad spectacle of broken homes and shattered lives. Divorce rates among Seventh-day Adventists do not differ significantly from divorce rates among worldlings.

Bickering, backbiting, and malicious gossip go on unabated. The grasping covetousness and overreaching in trade is very much with us. Some have even been known to brag about having "skinned" someone in a business deal. The terrible testimony of youths and adults entangled in sex, drugs, booze, and all the music and madness of their worldly contemporaries is a jarring reality. As a people we have often blended in with the worldly woodwork. Too many Adventists wear the same jewelry, see the same movies, dance to the same tunes, and are generally caught up in the same whirl of pulse-pounding excitement. And this is not some isolated package of case histories. It is very real and very sad. The overall sweep of the current SDA scene has an alarming similarity with the old Israelitish drift—a strange fascination with heathen gods. Baal worship! Not literal Baal, of course, but his equivalent. With many self is secretly enshrined in the high places of the heart!

The Scriptures plainly teach that the last days before the second coming would see a recycling of the corruption of the antediluvians and the final days of Sodom. God has graciously warned that the line of distinction between His professed people and sin-lovers must be plain and clear, or the coming destruction will strike both with equal force.[5]

Ever since I became an Adventist, I have heard Matthew 24:14 quoted. We love this passage of Scripture. And yet I wonder if we really know what Jesus is saying here: "This gospel of the kingdom shall be preached in all the world for a witness unto all nations; and then shall the end come."

Somehow we have projected the notion that if we could just get into every country on the face of the earth and establish some SDA contact, this would fulfill our mission. Such a notion is as far removed from the truth as is the misconception of the disciples in Christ's day when they clung tenaciously to the false idea that He was going to establish an earthly kingdom.

The key word in this text is *witness*. But what is a witness? Believing and proclaiming the truth about the Sabbath? Telling people about the state of the dead or the second coming of Jesus? Passing out literature that explains the important doctrines we hold so dear?

"Our doctrines may be correct; we may hate false doctrine, and may not receive those who are not true to principles; we may labor with untiring energy; but even this is not sufficient. . . . A belief in the theory of the truth is not enough. To present this theory to unbelievers does not constitute you a witness for Christ."[6]

We face the danger of finding ourselves in the same spiritual cul-de-sac as the Jews in Christ's day. They were strict Sabbath-keeping, health-reforming, Bible-believing, "God-fearing" church members, but they crucified the Lord of glory!

"The greatest deception of the human mind in Christ's day was that a mere assent to the truth constitutes righteousness. . . . The same danger still exists. . . . Men may profess faith in the truth; but if it does not make them sincere, kind, patient, forbearing, heavenly-minded, it is a curse to its possessors, and through their influence it is a curse to the world."[7]

It is a horrible thought, but is it possible that some Seventh-day Adventist could become a curse to the world?

How well I remember the evening a minister backhanded his son and sent him sprawling because he was noisy as vespers began. When a father shouts, "Shut up, you kids! We're going to have family worship!" the curse begins to take shape. In the case of the minister's son it came as no great surprise to me to learn a few years later that he had left the church, bitter against his parents, the denomination, and God Himself. This did not happen because of one isolated incident, but from an accumulated pattern of misrepresenting the character of God.

Back in the early 1950s my wife and I and our two daughters visited a small, back-country church tucked neatly in the foothills. It was one of those churches where it seems that everyone is somehow related to everyone else. We were true visitors. We sat about midway down the aisle with a lot of empty pews both ahead and behind us. The old potbellied stove in the rear was doing its best to generate some semblance of heat, but not really succeeding too well. The Sabbath School superintendent smiled and welcomed us to Sabbath School.

"I'm sorry," he apologized, "the stove isn't as hot as it should be on this cold morning. The person who was supposed to start the fire didn't start it on time."

From the rear of the room roared a loud, irate voice. "I DID TOO start the fire on time!"

"You did NOT!" yelled the superintendent from the pulpit.

"I DID TOO!"

"DID NOT!"

We were caught in the crossfire. Welcome to Sabbath School!

One of the single most prevalent Adventist cliches is the term, "finishing the work." I have heard that ever since those days on Okinawa, and I wonder if we honestly know what such a term means. Just suppose it were possible to baptize every man, woman, and child in the entire world—all the Protestants, Roman Catholics, Greek Orthodox, Jews, Moslems, Buddhists, Confucianists, Animists, Taoists, Hindus, Shintoists, and any other "ism" or idolater and atheist on the face of the globe. Imagine their all becoming Seventh-day Adventists! (It staggers the mind just figuring out the tithe and contemplating the rush on "vege" food.) But let's say they are all baptized church members of the Adventist faith. I am totally convinced that, even if such a thing should ever happen, "the work" would not necessarily be finished!

I made this statement from the pulpit once, and afterward a doctor met me at the door and said, "What you preached today is heresy." Then taking me by my coat lapels he pulled me closer. "But it's the truth!" he whispered loudly.

Now I certainly believe in baptism, but not as an end in itself, as if some statistical body count for a mythological "progress report" demonstrates that somehow the work is being finished. Too long have we subscribed to the false notion that "bodies, bucks, and bricks" fulfill the great commission! When we come to the place that we understand our own message and translate it into practical godliness, others will take notice. Such a life will produce a genuine witness.

Several years ago the public relations director for the Southern Baptists wrote a letter to the General Conference department, then known as Public Relations, about an Adventist family he had known in his early years as a pastor. Here is what he said:

"The best public relations I have ever seen from the Seventh-day Adventists were the Culverhouses. This aged couple lived just 200 yards from my first pastorate. They were convinced Seventh-day Adventists, but they were also good neighbors. They carried their share of community responsibility. They opened their humble home to the itinerant young pastor just as did the Baptists. They sent their tithe to their closest church nearly a hundred miles away, but they gave also to the little Baptist church to keep the gospel alive in their community. Some of the most elevating prayers I have ever heard were from Mr. Culverhouse. I can see him now, white hair, bowed head, on his knees. Once when the church had a storm sweep through it, the one force that helped the young pastor to keep his feet on the ground was the integrity and simple logic of this dedicated farmer. In that community, where he was the sole representative of his faith to which he was devoted publicly and privately, the name Seventh-day Adventist stood for something—integrity, dedication, loyalty to the Bible, common sense, good neighbor.

"We can have surveys, opinion research, planned campaigns, and all the rest, but we will never beat the kind of public relations I saw in Charlie Culverhouse. God bless his memory."

How wonderful when someone leaves such a track of light leading to God! How warm and good to find Seventh-day Adventists who are "seven days" Adventists; who do not distort the message with their free-swinging, worldly stamp or come across as gaunt and grim in their misguided zeal to live health reform if it kills them. What a privilege to know that there are magnetic Adventists who draw folk to Christ instead of repelling them!

At the present time we are in a transition period—between dying policies and programs and a primitive godliness waiting to be born. Jesus, speaking in Acts 1:8, gave us the key to understanding what God means by a witness to all the world.

"You will receive power when the Holy Spirit comes on you, and then you will be my witnesses not only in Jerusalem but throughout Judaea and Samaria, and indeed to the ends of the earth." Jerusalem Bible.

The Greek word for power in this verse is *dunamis*. It is from this word that Alfred Nobel derived the name for the powerful explosive he developed, which we call dynamite. God has promised to fill us with "dynamite"—explosive power if you please—in order to accomplish the work of heralding God's last message to every nation, kindred, tongue, and people in every quarter of the earth. I used to read this passage and wonder just how the word *dynamite* applied. But later, after a very revealing experience with the explosive, I understood more clearly.

Back in 1960 I purchased some property high in the Black Hills of western Washington. It had a fabulous, sweeping view of the snow-capped peaks of the Cascade Range. It was a wonderful spot. Nothing seemed to mar the beauty except for one thing. The whole hillside was dotted with huge, burned-over, head-high fir stumps. There was enough cleared area to build a house, but I fully intended to rid the whole hill of those unsightly black "monsters." I asked a friend of mine just how to go about such a task.

"You've got to blast them out," he declared.

With his promise to teach me how to use dynamite, I bought a case of the explosives, a coil of fuse, and a box of blasting caps, and began.

I was still blowing stumps long after we had moved into our little Swiss chalet. Then one summer day my wife said, "We have so many visitors coming to our hill, especially those with children. I just wish you'd get rid of the dynamite stored down there in the old barn. I'll plant ivy over the rest of the stumps. Now that it's getting warm I think it's just too dangerous to have it around."

She was right. Warm weather does change dynamite. A sudden jar can set off an unexpected cataclysm.

"Ok," I answered, "I'll get rid of the stuff. You and the girls stay indoors, and I'll make one final blast."

For many months I had had my eye on one huge old "beast" by the driveway. Every time I passed it in my car I would say, "Some day, baby, you're coming out of there!" I had singled out this stump because of its monstrous twelve-foot diameter base and proximity to the driveway.

I brought up the rest of the dynamite from the barn and proceeded to dig under the stump to lay the charge. After priming the first stick I began packing others around it. I knew the usual eight-to-ten sticks would not be enough, so I kept packing . . . 15, 20, 25, 30, 35, 40 . . . 50! I crammed in 50 sticks! There weren't any more sticks in the case! Then I reeled off 15 feet of fuse to allow plenty of time to get far away.

I lit the fuse and shouted the usual, "Fire in the hole," three times. Only this time I added to myself. "And I *mean* there is a fire in the hole!"

I'll have to admit I walked a bit faster than usual this time. I wanted to reach the top of Coyote Ridge, where I could watch the fireworks. From up there I could easily see our little chalet on the knoll not more than a hundred feet from the stump. Whisps of telltale smoke emerged from the ground. As the fuse burned steadily toward the charge I had a feeling that the whole hillside was going to blow shortly.

And just about then it happened. A terrific explosion rocked the ground and sent dirt, dust, and debris flying in all directions. For a moment the view of my house was obliterated by the upheaval. But I blinked like the proverbial toad in a hailstorm. I could not believe what I was seeing. The stump barely jiggled, then settled back down.

I hurried down the ridge to see what had happened. The smell of high explosive was still heavy in the air, but there before my wondering eyes was a huge cave blown clear out from under the stump. The earth had been blasted away, leaving nothing but a great cave, so huge I could actually crawl under the stump. But the stump still stood! The only thing that had been removed was dirt. I had far more fire power than necessary. I could have blown up a bridge with that much dynamite, BUT IT WASN'T PLACED IN THE RIGHT SPOT! I should have placed it squarely under "the beast" so the power of the explosion could have effectively dislodged it. Instead I just blew sod!

I went back to Acts 1:8. The promise for power is there. God's Spirit can blast loose all the evil traits and clear us from our own carnality, but we must be willing to allow Him to place that power in the *right spot*—in our hearts!

If dynamite must be placed in the right spot for its power to be effective, how much more is this true of the power of the Holy Spirit. It is not enough just to know the message of Jesus Christ. It is not enough to attend a Christian school and get a diploma, to march down the aisle with honors to the tune of "Pomp and Circumstance." It is not enough to keep learning and learning until there is a whole disarranged alphabet after one's name. It is not enough merely to share our unique message with others. The Holy Spirit must translate that message into practical godliness. Otherwise we are just blowing sod!

Two little six-year-old girls attended church in their spring finery. Both had reached the age when the front teeth were missing, and the tongue protruded through the gap. Any conversation at close range usually meant getting sprayed.

One of the girls sidled up to her companion to make an announcement. "The memory verth for today ith, 'Be ye kind one to another,' " she lisped smugly.

The other girl shook her head. "Ith not either!" she lisped back. Not understanding the King James Version, she proceeded to quote, "Ith 'Be 'E kind one to another.' " And as she said this the little feather that angled so cutely from her new hat danced in unison with her shaking head.

"Ith not either. Ith 'Be YE kind!' "

" 'Be 'E kind!' " the other countered.

Little "Be ye kind" became so angry that she tore the feather from her challenger's hat, threw it to the floor, and stomped on it. That did it. Instantly they began clawing and scratching each other in a first-class, mini-female fight in church. And the irony of it all was that it was over the memory verse "Be ye kind one to another"! These little girls were just blowing sod!

Now listen to the following statement: "The reason why our people have not more power is that they profess the truth, but do not practice it."[8] Could it be that like my misplaced dynamite and those two little girls, many of us are just blowing sod?

Our greatest need today is for a true revival and reformation. In the days of young King Josiah it was brought about by the discovery of the book of the law. That ancient scroll had been buried amidst the clutter of the sanctuary itself. What followed was an unprecedented reformation and destruction of idols.

Could it be that we need once again to discover the message of those three angels given especially to us in Revelation 14:6-12? We have systematically printed their figures on letterheads, used them as a logo on our literature, and sculptured statuary of these angels flying in the midst of heaven, but do we know what they mean to us individually?

There has been a sinister plot against these messages. It has been Satan's studied purpose to cause the remnant people to accept only a superficial understanding of what those three angels were shouting about so loudly in John's vision.[9]

Day by day we are moving into line—moving toward the point of no return—the final separation between those who are controlled by God and those who are manipulated by Satan. Decisions are being made today for time and eternity.

"As we near the close of earth's history, we either rapidly advance in Christian growth, or we rapidly retrograde toward the world."[10] As the saying goes, You will be tomorrow what you are becoming today!

It was almost noon on the last Saturday of March 1955. A crippled Pan American Airways Stratocruiser went down 25 miles off the Oregon coast. All 23 persons aboard the ditched aircraft survived the crash. A *Seattle Times* newspaper reporter picked up the drama and wrote this account:

"It was what they call a calm sea. The ocean winds were almost noiseless. The men and women in the life rafts could talk clearly to those who were about to die. . . . Those in the rafts who had strength paddled, and those in the water swam, but the sea was stronger than all. . . .'For as long as perhaps a half hour,' said one survivor, 'we stroked, and they swam, and called for help, but we couldn't gain an inch.' . . . Soundlessly, remorselessly, the rolling sea separated those who would live from those who would die. . . . The three in the ocean drifted away until the last cry for help was heard across the expanding gulf of salt water."[11]

What a tragedy! The sea and elements finally took their toll on those three bobbing in their life jackets! They died from exposure even while being supported on the waves. It is hard to understand how someone could be lost while wearing his life jacket. But some will be lost right within the church, right where they could easily learn how to keep from perishing. This, however, need not happen.

This book is a new, fresh look at those three angels' messages and how God designed them to prepare us for that grand event of meeting Christ face to face when He returns.

---

1. See Ellen G. White, *Testimonies for the Church*, vol. 7, p. 138.
2. *Ibid*., vol. 5, pp. 75, 76.
3. *Ibid*., p. 160.

4. *Ibid.*, p. 217.

5. See *Ibid.*, vol. 1, p. 189.

6. Ellen G. White, *Review and Herald*, February 2, 1891, emphasis supplied.

7. Ellen G. White, *The Desire of Ages*, pp. 309, 310.

8. *Testimonies*, vol. 4, p. 613.

9. See Ellen G. White, *Selected Messages*, bk. 2, p. 117.

10. White, *Review and Herald,* December 13, 1892.

11. Excerpts from the *Seattle Times*, March 30, 1955.

"I saw another angel fly in the midst of heaven, having the everlasting gospel to preach unto them that dwell on the earth, and to every nation, and kindred, and tongue, and people." Revelation 14:6.

Born on Death Row

On a Sabbath day many centuries ago, John the beloved was carried off in vision. The barrenness of rocky Patmos faded from view, and suddenly the aged apostle was transported in spirit to heaven, where he saw, heard, and felt things beyond the realm of normal human experience. Ushered into the very throne room of God, he beheld a glorified Christ. Repeatedly John heard angels shouting utterances that dealt with the theme of the great controversy between Christ and Satan clear down to the end of time. Then in Revelation 14 John describes the scene of another angel flying in the midst of heaven, this time carrying the "everlasting gospel."

Now angels were never commissioned to preach the gospel. This has been reserved as a high privilege for man. Angels, however, have appeared in human form, assisting humanity in the work of telling the good news. These heavenly messengers have always been a means of communication between heaven and earth, but they have never experienced what it means to be lost and finally rescued. Their reaction to the preaching of the good news has ever been one of fascination. "These are things," writes Peter, "that angels long to see into." 1 Peter 1:12, NEB.

As with most of the book of Revelation, we are dealing with highly symbolic language. The first, second, and third angels that John saw flying in Revelation 14 symbolize the task of human beings who will proclaim their messages.[1]

25

Those angels represent us! Their flight path through the heavens suggests the global nature of the work God has commissioned to us to do.

This is the only place in the Bible where *everlasting* is associated with the gospel.[2] It is the eternal good news. There is only one gospel to save men. There will never be another, because there is only one Saviour. The tombs of all other would-be saviours are still occupied, but Jesus' sepulchre is empty!

When God gave Adam and Eve a simple test of obedience His words must have sounded strange. "In the day that thou eatest thereof thou shalt surely die." But what was death? Nowhere in this fresh new world, nor in the entire universe, had death ever been seen. The very word sounded ominous, yet death at that point in time could not be fully grasped. But after sin entered a change came, and both Adam and Eve watched sadly as the first leaf fell from a stately tree. They observed this phenomenon with inexpressible sorrow. We are told that "as they witnessed in drooping flower and falling leaf the first signs of decay, Adam and his companion mourned more deeply than men now mourn over their dead."[3]

Some time ago I stood beside the grave of a four-year-old lad and wept bitterly at the sight of his small casket. It wrenched my heart. I have known the even more numbing anguish of standing beside the grave of my own beautiful twenty-four-year-old daughter, and have felt the lacerating pains that clawed at my heart. But imagine attending a funeral for a mere leaf! Yet, as the tears trickled down the cheeks of Adam and Eve, they felt the most poignant sorrow over what was happening to their beautiful world, especially the lofty trees. Death was upon them now. It was visible and oppressive. It would become a painful, heart-rending experience when they lost their son Abel!

Sin is the embodiment of disobedience and disloyalty; it frequently displays itself in utter selfishness. We often talk about "innocent" babies, and in a certain sense, of course, they are innocent. But place two of them in a crib with one rattle, and it won't be long before they are beating each other over the head with it!

Sin entered the world because our first parents pledged allegiance to Satan. The devil had promised that their eyes would be opened if they transgressed. Their eyes were indeed opened—opened to all the misery and heartache and death that only sin can bring! But more than this it brought guilt. And guilt is a killer. Its knowledge makes people afraid. They want to hide. This is precisely the kind of knowledge God did not want our first parents to have. It shatters real communication and destroys relationships.

Several years ago a rather revealing survey was conducted at a boarding academy with an enrollment of approximately 400 students. The first question asked was, "How would you like to have Jesus as your roommate or living across the hall?" Only 25 percent of the student body desired to have Jesus that near. Second question: "Why?" And without exception the answer centered around guilt. There were books, magazines, hidden drugs, tobacco, booze, language, and life-styles that made these teenagers feel most uncomfortable at the thought of having Jesus physically so nearby.

In the Boston Art Museum a striking picture hangs in the religious section of the gallery. I have often stood back and squinted at it, because from a distance it actually seems like two pictures. Off to the right the scenery depicting paradise is bathed in sunshine, with great lofty trees, colorful vines, and flowers blooming everywhere. But to the left all is dark and sinister. Upon closer examination two lonely figures in animal skins slink away from the garden down an obscure path, pressed tightly against an overhanging cliff. Beasts of prey lurk in the shadows. A waterfall splashes spray as the guilty pair seem headed into an approaching storm. For me the painting has always depicted a real sense of the fall.

But even beyond guilt there is worse to come. "Sin not only shuts away from God, but destroys in the human soul both the desire and the capacity for knowing Him."[4]

A strange blindness sets in: wrong looks right and right

looks wrong. Confusion settles over the whole human scene like a bad London fog. After presenting the good news of the Saviour to someone, how often have I heard the sad words, "Well, I just don't know."

Sin brings on a derangement, and the mind, twisted by a perverted imagination, becomes so corrupt that even the high and lofty attributes of God are misinterpreted and His gracious actions misunderstood. His justice and majesty are considered cruel. His love and mercy are translated to mean sentimental weakness.

Sin has a way of depraving the will itself, polluting and debasing the very heart of man. A numbing of the understanding and a consistent resistance to spiritual things paralyzes. Gradually the very thought patterns become hardened and insensitive to the gospel message. A nonresponse surfaces, even when the Holy Spirit comes in His mighty power, seeking to convict and convert. Death! Like a severed branch from the living tree, the person shrivels away in his own self-centeredness.

And yet, in spite of all these factors, sin has a way of looking exciting and downright alluring. That is what makes it so damnably dangerous. The outright attractiveness and appeal merits its being classified as "the mystery of iniquity." Alexander Pope touched the very heart of the problem, when he wrote these lines:

> Vice is a monster of so frightful mein,
> As to be hated needs but to be seen;
> Yet seen too oft, familiar with her face,
> We first endure, then pity, then embrace.

Humanity doesn't seem to get enough vice and violence in the sickening daily news, so it turns to more of it in the form of so-called "entertainment"! A good chunk of TV and film fare is largely based on the creative expression of carnality. The more stimulating, the bigger the box-office returns. Depicting depravity promoted as quality productions creates an illusion of normalcy. Thus humanity, feeding on the husks, finds no taste for that which is pure, honest, or true concerning God.

The sin problem is so all-pervasive, so total, that there is no human way to escape it. We are all born on death row! Without a Saviour we would live out our sordid little lives and die without hope.

Back in the late 1950s while I was working on a photo-feature assignment at a state penitentiary for the rotogravure section of a large city newspaper, I was thrust into the full significance of the meaning of death row. I had finished my interior work of interviews and shots of cellblocks and work area, when I stepped outside to wrap up the shooting of the exterior. It was then that I spotted a strange protrusion on one of the walls. The room looked windowless. I inquired about the reason for this and was informed that it was the hanging chamber. The cellblock next to this room housed the dreaded death row, where prisoners waited their turn to die. I was forbidden to take pictures of all this, but a guard volunteered to give me full details.

Inside the hanging chamber there are thirteen steps leading up to the spring-loaded trap door. Two large hooks hang from the ceiling. These are used for instances when the state has scheduled a double execution. A small partition to the left of this room contains a few seats for visitors, a glass for viewing the hanging, and an electric panel with three matching switches. On the day of the execution an electrician is flown in from out of town. He rewires the switches and leaves. He is the only one who knows which switch is "hot."

When the death hour comes and the condemned person is led in, a minister offers a final prayer. The criminal is led up the steps to the platform, a hood is placed over his head, and the noose is snugly tightened around his neck. When all appears ready, the warden, watching through the glass, gives the nod and three guards approach the switches. At the given signal they simultaneously press a button. The hot switch activates the trap door, which springs open, and the prisoner drops to his death.

But what if someone in that visitor's room should suddenly step forward and cry out, "I'll take that man's place!"

Such an act should be headline news even in this jaded, old world. The news media would disseminate it everywhere—someone willingly accepting death for another person! But as the apostle Paul so eloquently put it, "In human experience it is a rare thing for one man to give his life for another, even if the latter be a good man, though there have been a few who have had the courage to do it. Yet the proof of God's amazing love is this: that it was while we were sinners that Christ died for us." Romans 5:7, 8, Phillips.

Even such high drama as a substitute paying the death penalty for someone else fails adequately to sound the depths of what Christ did that Friday afternoon on Golgotha. He experienced eternal death—total separation from God. And He did this on behalf of every person who has ever lived or who will ever live on this planet! At that time it seemed to Him that the depths of sin were so profound that He would never again see His Father's face. The horror of that "black hole" appeared so dark and deep and eternal that it crushed out His life. For Him at that moment there was no bright hope of a resurrection; only the depths of an abyss beyond the comprehension of any mortal.

But He arose victorious over death! And that, even after all these centuries, is the good news! Good news because Christ by conquering death has provided the sure promise that all who accept Him will be raised from the dead or translated to heaven without seeing death. On that glad day we shall see our friends and loved ones again!

Christ's death and resurrection is good news because He has destroyed the works of the devil and proven him to be a liar. Through Christ's power we *can* overcome every inherited and cultivated tendency to sin. We can be freed from our pride and passions. Jesus came to deliver His people from their sins, not in them. He never told the woman caught in adultery to "go and taper off." No, he said, "Go and sin no more." Surely it is good news that He can keep us from falling and present us faultless before the throne.

It is certainly good news that we can be forgiven our sins and placed back on the path to the kingdom. Good news it is that we have a Representative in the heavenly court who can plead our case against the charges of the enemy. Good news that He is our Elder Brother, who will ever bear the marks of sin and who understands all our temptations, problems, and pains, and is no farther away than our next heartbeat. Good news that with such closeness He can handle all the damaging charges that are brought against us by the accusing enemy who tempts us to sin and then delights to accuse us when we fall.

And most certainly it is good news that Christ is coming again and that His coming will bring a halt to sin and suffering. The entire, onlooking universe will at last be placed on an eternally secure basis because of Him.

Even though we all have been born on death row, the good news provides the promise that we can be set free, eternally free! That is why John's vision of angels flying in mid-heaven carrying the everlasting good news leaps out as so significant. No wonder it has such a world-wide urgency!

---

1. See *Testimonies*, vol. 6, p. 17.
2. See *Seventh-day Adventist Bible Commentary*, vol. 7, p. 827.
3. Ellen G. White, *Patriarchs and Prophets*, p. 62.
4. Ellen G. White, *Prophets and Kings*, p. 233.

"Saying with a loud voice, Fear God." Revelation 14:7.

Fear That Is Unafraid

As in other passages of Revelation, the angels shout or give their messages in a loud voice that we may know the importance God places upon them. There is a logical progression in what the angels say, and these first two words, "fear God," need to be understood because they lay the foundation for all man's relationships to his Maker and to other men.

The tyranny of words often prevents us from honestly understanding the meaning of what we desire to convey. The word *fear* is one of these. It has both a negative and positive element in it, as we shall see.

I well remember being invited to attend a Sabbath afternoon Bible study session with a group of college students. They came to the first two words of the first angel's message, "fear God," and after four hours they still felt that they had not sounded the depths of its meaning. They had learned something of the ambivalence this word contains.

Most people think of fear in relationship to dread, fright, dismay, panic, terror, or some negative emotional state. Many people have illogical fears of various kinds. These may range from acrophobia to xenophobia. For instance, I have a touch of claustrophobia—fear of closed or narrow spaces. As a documentary film maker I am always interested in knowing what other cinematographers go through when they take their shots. When I heard about one who went a mile deep in a coal mine and crawled a half mile back through a space 18 inches high to do his filming of a coal-mining operation, I shuddered. The pay would have to be very high to get me to wiggle through such a place! Also I don't especially enjoy high places. No amount of money can lure me to stand on the girder of a building or a high preci-pice to film a scene or do anything else for that matter. Acro-phobia is such a part of me that I have a hard enough time inching up to an overlook, even if it has a railing. Most other people have similar fears of one kind or another.

For lack of a better single word we sometimes combine the word *fear* with another word to modify the concept. We speak of having a "healthy fear," for instance. Learning to keep our hands off hot stoves is an example of this kind of fear.

Years ago I heard a lecture by a mountain rescue expert who was the first person ever to climb the north face of Mount Rainier in winter. He told of the narrow ledge where he and four of his teammates "slept" the first night sitting back to back. Then he related how easy it was to lean over and spit down 4,000 feet! But don't get the wrong idea. This alpinist had a healthy fear or respect for the old mountain. Later, when some young "bucks" fresh out of college spied him roped up while crossing a "gentle" glacier, they teased him about the extra safety precautions he took. "Why did you bother to rope up?" they jibed. "Because I want to get back!" he replied.

The way the Scriptures use the word *fear* shows that it has a range of meanings. This is not unusual. Take the word *wine,* for instance. It can mean more than one thing. Isaiah, for example, speaks of the new wine "found in the cluster," (Isaiah 65:8), or bunch of grapes. In other words, grape juice. On the other hand, Solomon speaks of wine that "sparkles in the cup," but which "in the end . . . bites like a snake." Proverbs 23:31, 32, NIV. The latter writer is obvi-ously referring to something a little stronger than grape juice.

Fully to understand this word *fear* as used in the Bible depends on the meaning God intended to convey and the one to whom it applies. Thus, "fear God" has a different meaning to the sinner than it does to the saint. The sinner, in rebellion against God and all He stands for, will eventually know the real meaning of terror, because "it is a fearful thing to fall into the hands of the living God." Hebrews 10:31. But to the Christian saint, who rests his hope in the promises and love of the Saviour, "fear God" means awesome respect and reverence for the Deity we serve. This latter is the kind of fear that is not afraid.

From this it is evident that when Christians use the expression, "fear God," they don't always mean the same thing. Thus, for instance, the Scriptures teach that God is readily accessible (see Acts 17:27) and that we are to "come boldly [with confidence] unto the throne of grace" (Hebrews 4:16), yet this accessibility is balanced by the awesomeness of God's presence which leaves man prostrate (see 1 Timothy 6:16; Ezekiel 1:28). The Scriptures point up this variety of meaning in such texts as these:

"There is no fear in love; but perfect love casteth out fear: because fear hath torment." 1 John 4:18.

"They that feared the Lord spake often one to another." Malachi 3:16.

The children of Israel trembled when Heaven's "fire power" was displayed on Sinai. Never before nor since has the world witnessed anything so awe-inspiring as when God the Father stood beside His Son while giving the law. The Bible says that even Moses, the man of God, was affected. "And so terrible was the sight, that Moses said, I exceedingly fear and quake." Hebrews 12:21.

Obviously the Israelites experienced something of the "terror of the Lord." 2 Corinthians 5:11. This sort of fear is something different from the groveling, panic-stricken terror the last rebellious sinners will one day experience. See Revelation 6:16, 17. Godly fear is the beginning of wisdom. It is based on a realization of the character, greatness, and majesty of God and of one's own unworthiness.

When Christ comes the second time, the ambivalence of this term will again be apparent. Jeremiah graphically portrays the time-of-trouble experience: "Thus saith the Lord; We have heard a voice of trembling, of fear, and not of peace. . . . Alas! for that day is great, so that none is like it: it is even the time of Jacob's trouble; but he shall be saved out of it." Jeremiah 30:5-7.

Yet out of this in-depth soul searching prior to Jesus' return there will come a rejoicing that is beyond our wildest imagination today. "It shall be said in that day, Lo, this is our God; we have waited for him, and he will save us: this is the Lord; we have waited for him, we will be glad and rejoice in his salvation." Isaiah 25:9. Here again is fear that is not afraid.

When we understand the sinfulness of sin we begin to grasp why this ambivalence exists. It is for this reason that the Israelites reacted as they did at the base of Mount Sinai. They caught a glimpse of their own sinfulness when they realized they were in the very presence of Deity. We must ever remember that our God is a God of love, but that He hates sin, hates it so much that He intends ultimately to destroy every particle of it from His universe. He intends to cleanse and purify all things. He will destroy sin outside of us, if we will let Him; but He must destroy us with it, if we refuse to give it up.

It is this prospect that causes those who know God to fear lest they harbor some cherished sin in their lives. This is the kind of fear that the prophets experienced. This is the kind of fear Isaiah felt, after seeing the Lord high and lifted up. He records that he fell on his face crying, "Woe is me! for I am undone; because I am a man of unclean lips." Isaiah 6:5.

Satan has always tried to capitalize on the nature of our sin-hating God. When people react negatively to his tyrant theme, he thrusts before them the opposite extreme, that God is too good to destroy sinners.

But this is not Satan's only strategy for leading souls captive. He loves to humanize and sentimentalize the God of the universe through music, art, and literature. Satan well knows that any lessening of God as He really is brings man down to a god of his own devising. Today we are inundated by a tidal wave of sentimentalism that cheapens sacred things. It runs the gamut from bumper stickers ("Honk if you love Jesus") to so-called religious words tacked on to music appropriate for the night club or "Joe's Barroom." Performers swing and sway, seemingly nursing microphones, crooning to the savage beat of some sentimental love song, but substituting, of course, the name of Jesus for the "lover" in the song—and then they think they are honoring or elevating that sacred name!

Our deportment before God should be characterized by humility and reverence. It is true that we may come with confidence into His presence, but we must never approach Him as if He were on a level with ourselves. There are those today who talk to the great and all-powerful Majesty of heaven, who dwells in an atmosphere of brilliant, unapproachable light, as if they were chatting with an equal or even an inferior.[1]

"Let us have grace, whereby we may serve God acceptably with reverence and godly fear: for our God is a consuming fire." Hebrews 12:28, 29.

Once we catch the significance of God's hatred of sin, we can understand what is meant by "godly fear." There will ever remain a proper and awesome respect for Deity, yet at the same time we will be drawn heavenward by God's Spirit because Christ is our Elder Brother and God is our Father. We shall have fear without being afraid.

True wisdom and knowledge both start here. "The fear of the Lord" is both "the beginning of wisdom" and "the beginning of knowledge." Psalm 111:10; Proverbs 1:7. The tragic history of ancient Israel stemmed largely from a lack of reverential fear. As a result they lost both the wisdom and knowledge of God. When first settling in Canaan, they acknowledged the principles of the theocracy and correspondingly prospered, because God was their king. But gradually, imperceptibly they began to adopt the customs and habits of their heathen neighbors, and in so doing sacrificed their own peculiar high calling. Without realizing it they lost their reverence for God, and once that happened, it wasn't long before they "ceased to prize the honor of being His chosen people."[2]

Adventists have long seen their counterpart in ancient Israel. The matter of reverence ought to alert us to the unconscious departure from true worship. The lax behavior of many in modern Israel demonstrates far too often that they simply have not grapsed the significance of the expression "fear God." Borrowing questionable customs from other churches, many of us secularize our services with announcements that border on clubhouse promotions and degenerate into fund-raising ballyhoo, ranging from Pathfinder "bike-a-thons" to Investment sales.

Once in a large suburban church I actually witnessed an Investment leader hold up a branch of cherries. Obviously caught up in the worthy-cause syndrome, he enthusiastically gave a promotional sales pitch. "We're selling these cherries for 23 cents a pound," he announced, "and that's five cents cheaper than any market around here. You can get them after Sabbath."

Suddenly I got what could be termed "ecclesiastical whiplash." My mind snapped from worship to the weekly routine of buying and selling.

Under the guise of the "King's business" we often intrude into our worship services announcements that have little or nothing to do with the King, only some well-meaning but wholly inappropriate project and our own churchy affairs. We love to see ourselves as real go-getters, pacing ourselves in the religious fast lane. But in so doing we rob ourselves and our children of the blessings of genuine worship.

Once I even witnessed a series of announcements that took the entire eleven o'clock service. The pastor began preaching at noon! His otherwise effective and powerful sermon from the Word was lost. The weary congregation long since had been turned off and tuned out by the arm-waving, show-and-tell promotionals that preceded the sermon.

On another occasion something similar happened at one of our larger gatherings, and the speaker, a General Conference official, felt impressed to administer a firm rebuke for such goings on. Immediately after being introduced he stood and raising his hands, said solemnly, "The congregation will please rise for the benediction!"

When announcements are carefully screened (ideally not repeated from the church newsletter or bulletin) and are made prior to the actual worship period, a more worshipful attitude is usually shown by most congregations.

Whispering and common conversation, no matter how friendly, is not worship either. Only one hour a week is devoted to the worship service, and the sanctuary is intended to be a place to meet with our God. It is not the place for visiting, nor is it the place for applause.

The habit of applauding a sacred number, as if the musician were some secular performer offering expertise in religious entertainment, is totally inappropriate for worship. Perhaps the little girl who was interviewed by Art Linkletter on his TV show a number of years ago captured it best when she declared sweetly that she was an Adventist.

"And what makes Adventists different?" asked Mr. Linkletter.

"Oh, we're noisier!" she declared.

In our irreverence we are the losers. "Our present habits and customs, which dishonor God and bring the sacred and heavenly down to the level of the common, are against us."[3]

Where is the dynamite of divine power these days? Perhaps it is lost in our irreverence, which we have not detected either individually or collectively. "The evils that have been gradually creeping in among us have imperceptibly led individuals and churches away from reverence for God, and have shut away the power which He desires to give them."[4]

When we truly fear God, we enter into a fellowship with Heaven that lifts us above the strife and stress of this life. But more than this, it shuts us in by His majesty and power, and we are never afraid of what puny man threatens to do or seemingly can do to hurt us. God has said, "I will never leave thee nor forsake thee." So that we may boldly say, "The Lord is my helper, and I will not fear what man shall do unto me." Hebrews 13:5, 6. When we fear God in the sense of respecting and honoring Him we are placed on heaven's angelic guardian list. "The angel of the Lord encampeth round about them that fear him, and delivereth them." Psalm 34:7.

The fear of the Lord releases us from all other fears. He who stands in awe of God can be free from all other anxieties. He does not worry about a financial crisis or a nuclear war. Wars and rumors of war do not shake us; neither do personal or family problems. Those who "commit the keeping of their souls . . . as unto a faithful Creator" (1 Peter 4:19), who knows how to make way for tomorrow, find rest in trusting Him completely.

When perplexities or stressful situations arise, we can go directly and with confidence to the One who understands the depths of our own hearts. The finite can always find strength in the Infinite! This is what Moses wanted so much to leave with the Israelites in his last speech to them before he headed up to Nebo to die. "The eternal God is thy refuge," he said, "and underneath are the everlasting arms." Deuteronomy 33:27.

Reverence, then, is the root and mainspring of all piety and is certainly a mighty deterrent to sin of any description, for "by the fear of the Lord men depart from evil." Proverbs 16:6. True reverence inevitably leads to obedience.

Is it any wonder then that the first two words of the first angel's message are "fear God"? It prepares us for what is to come during the third angel's message, when all the world will be arrayed against God's people. We shall fear and yet be unafraid!—fear to do anything that will displease God, yet be unafraid of what man can do to us. Those two words convey the thought of absolute loyalty to the One who will see His people through because they have made a full surrender to His will.

---

1. See *Patriarchs and Prophets*, p. 252.
2. *Patriarchs and Prophets*, p. 603.
3. *Testimonies*, vol. 5, p. 495.
4. *Ibid.*, p. 711.

"Give glory to him." Revelation 14:7.

Wanted: Dead, Not Alive

"Give glory to him" emerges as one of the most difficult passages in Scripture, because it requires people to take the words from their mouths and honestly put them into their hearts. Giving God the glory touches the tender nerve ends of our pride. It is the very heart of all reform and means, quite frankly, a total destruction to self-worship. Any theology that seeks to satisfy the senses or in any way sanctions self-indulgence or pride is not the religion of Christ and ought to be suspect.

Human pride rests at the bottom of all heathen religions. The notion that man can do something for merit lies at the foundation of all idolatry. Throughout history Satan's efforts have been a consistent pattern of seeking to saturate the church with this philosophy. "Whenever [this principle] is held, men have no barrier against sin."[1] Men will rise no higher than their concept of righteousness. J. B. Phillips captures this concept well in his paraphrased version of 2 Corinthians 10:12: "Of course we shouldn't dare include ourselves in the same class as those who write their own testimonials, or even to compare ourselves with them! All they are doing, of course, is to measure themselves by their own standards or by comparisons within their own circle, and that doesn't make for accurate estimation, you may be sure."

Pride is the cholesterol that plugs up the free flow of the gospel. The Madison Avenue approach to God's message has far too often fostered the very evils which His Word condemns. Are we religiously successful only when people praise us? From our earliest days we have been awarded buttons, ribbons, pins, and plaques for doing, saying, singing, distributing, and studying, but for whose glory? "Ego-trip" witnessing is ever popular.

Whole conferences get swept up in this tide. In the early 1970s I responded quickly when I heard an eloquent plea for a specialized prison ministry. A mature woman was needed to hold Bible studies in the women's ward at the state penitentiary. I finally found a dedicated Christian woman who was willing, along with a close friend of hers, to hold those Bible studies every weekend. But to my dismay their ministry was refused, not because these women lacked any qualifications but because their membership was in an adjoining conference, and credit for any baptisms would not make the local register!

We love to inhale the deadly fumes of applause because it titillates our pride. My stint in the army included training in chemical warfare. Vials of slightly diluted deadly gas were passed around the room. The men were supposed to uncork the containers and take a small whiff. How well I remember the effect of smelling the new-mown-hay odor of deadly phosgene gas. I wanted so much to inhale deeply. Applause is like that fatal gas.

John Knox well understood the dangers. Once after the fiery old preacher had finished a sermon and stood at the church door shaking hands, a gushing dowager shook his hand, flattering him that he was certainly the best preacher in all Scotland. "Aye," Knox replied, "the devil told me that before I left the pulpit!"

No greater incongruity can be shown than a professed Christian seeking credit for himself rather than giving glory to God. You could see this in the early disciples when they argued over who should be accounted the greatest. Earthly thoughts, earthly motives, and the prospect of an earthly kingdom swept them along. The upper room experience that preceded Pentecost transformed all that. Only after this change could God work through them with His Spirit.

Today we are too often still in the arguing stage, competing and elbowing within the church. From local situations where someone gets miffed because he or she wasn't appointed to a particular office to entire conferences getting uptight over a fund-raising report or a baptismal body count which might be larger in another area.

We simply could not stand a resurrection! If Peter held our present attitude when he was instrumental in raising Dorcas to life, he would have told James excitedly, "Get this report in the *Nazareth News* and the *Jerusalem Journal*!" (But, of course, the miracle of that resurrection would never have happened had he held that attitude.)

The real stalwarts of the Bible would never have appeared on the scene of action had they been swept up in the contemporary public relations concept of expediency for popularity. The three Hebrews out there on the Plain of Dura at the bow-or-burn ceremony would have bent over to tie their sandals when the orchestra hit the high note. It would have been more prudent to pretend participation so they could have continued good relations with the king. After all, they could have reasoned, what good would they be scorched, when they had such a top standing with the monarch? The "cause" might suffer if they were killed.

And Daniel certainly would have closed those windows while praying three times a day. After all, it behooves a VIP to be discreet when holding such a high standing in the government. Persisting in a personal practice at a time when a den of lions waits as the only alternative certainly is not good public relations.

And so it would have gone, until all that would have been left for us to read would be the tragic history of flaccid followers of every whim that centered on image-building rather than on a strong relationship with the Lord that can endure any test.

Pride, of course, is only part of the problem. "The old sinful nature within us is against God. It never did obey God's laws and it never will." Romans 8:7, LB. Until there is a total willingness to let go and let God the sham of going through the motions of being a Christian will continue to negate the truth about Christ's ability to transform the life.

We can only glorify God by living daily in cooperation with the Holy Spirit. "You do not belong to yourselves but to God; he bought you for a price. So use your bodies for God's glory." 1 Corinthians 6:20, TEV. Since we are to glorify God in our bodies, it does affect everything we do—our business, conversation, dress, drinking, eating, reading, and recreation. We will not want any misunderstanding concerning whom we represent. "Whether therefore ye eat, or drink, or whatsoever ye do, do all to the glory of God." 1 Corinthians 10:31.

This kind of text makes many in our free-swinging society very nervous. Under the cover of that old cry of "legalism" is a consistent departure from the very standards and practices that are designed to uplift humanity. That right rules and regulations can be followed for wrong reasons always lurks in the shadows, but there ever remains the truth about daily living under the direction of God's Spirit.

"Christianity proposes a reformation in the heart. What Christ works within, will be worked out under the dictation of a converted intellect. The plan of beginning outside and trying to work inward has always failed, and will always fail. God's plan with you is to begin at the very seat of all difficulties, the heart, and then from out of the heart will issue the principles of righteousness; the reformation will be outward as well as inward."[2] If you tell people to take off their jewelry, they will wear it under their underwear! Indeed I have known that to happen in our schools. When we start inward, the glory goes to God, but if we start from the outside, the glory goes to ourselves.

"Don't let the world around you squeeze you into its own mold, but let God remold your minds from within, so that you may prove in practice that the plan of God for you is good, meets all his demands and moves toward the goal of true maturity." Romans 12:2, Phillips, original.

Often we are squeezed into the worldly mold by habits

that counter both physical and mental health, ranging from TV program selection and late hours to wrong food combinations and eating habits. "Conformity to the world is a sin which is sapping the spirituality of our people, and seriously interfering with their usefulness. It is idle to proclaim the warning message to the world, while we deny it in the transactions of daily life."[3]

When we become gloomy, despondent, grouchy, and irritable it is because self is allowed to rule in our lives. The very first camp meeting I ever attended had two large signs posted behind the counter at the location booth. One read "Are you ready for the time of trouble?" The other quoted Psalm 119:165, "Great peace have they which love thy law; and nothing shall offend them." After watching folk get huffy over tent locations, flooring, and bedding, I began to understand the wisdom of such reminders.

We all need reminders like that. A deacon was berating a teen-ager for some mistake he felt needed correcting. His protracted vigor kept up long after his point was made. On and on he went in a vitriolic outburst that beat down upon the youngster like some desolating hail. To his credit the teenager did not respond in kind, but slowly began walking around the deacon, eyeing him studiously from head to toe.

"Well, what are you looking for?" shouted the deacon.

"The love of Jesus," came the quiet reply.

Death to self is the only answer to unsanctified behavior. We often quote the verse "I die daily," little realizing its full significance. Suppose there were a funeral for Brother Doward. There I am serenely settled into the padded casket. Flanked by flowers and wreaths from those who have come to pay their last respects, I remain quietly in my silk-lined coffin, awaiting the final viewing. The organist plays some touching background music, and when the signal is given, my friends pass quietly by my remains. One of my former students whispers to a colleague, "You know, I never did like him as a teacher. He turned me off."

Suddenly a little frown creases my forehead. The former

student nudges his neighbor quickly and points excitedly. "I don't think he's dead!"

And about then someone else passes and whispers approvingly, "Doward was one of the best teachers and preachers I ever heard."

A slight smile curves my mouth. The procession halts. "You know, I don't think he's gone!" exclaims someone else.

And I certainly wouldn't be! Dead men do not respond. When we are truly dead to self we will be perfectly in harmony and at peace with God just as our Saviour was. "He was never elated by applause, nor dejected by censure or disappointment. Amid the greatest opposition and the most cruel treatment, He was still of good courage."[4]

"Why is it so hard to lead a self-denying, humble life? Because professed Christians are not dead to the world. It is easy living after we are dead."[5] Now that is a strange paradox—easy living—after we are dead! It is easy because a thousand things that now attract us or disturb us will never be noticed. We may be crucified with Christ, but we live a life so full of joy, so tranquil in His love, that we simply do not awaken to any self-centered stimulation.

Glorifying God is a joyful, happy experience. A life of total trust that lifts us above the petty problems and jarring strife is the outworking of meeting temptations with the promises of God to deliver, however thick and fast they may come. The sanctifying power of practicing a consistent prayer life leads to glorifying God. Every emergency is a call to prayer, and the inevitable result is peace and a true understanding of the Lord's Prayer—"for thine is the kingdom, and the power, and the glory, for ever." Matthew 6:13.

Several years ago I was asked to help with a Bible study group for about two dozen inmates at the state penitentiary. As we sat around the large table I leaned over and whispered to the inmate next to me, "It's nice to meet with fellow Christians."

He snorted and chuckled a little. "Oh, we're not all Christians here."

Since I was a bit naive about such matters, I raised my eyebrows. "But I thought because you brought your Bibles and—"

"Naw!" he cut me off. "Some of us just wanna get out of lock-up, that's all."

I gulped. "Well, surely there must be at least one Christian here."

"Yeah, there's a Christian here. Ya see that black guy sittin' clear in the back of the room—the one with the deep scar down his skull?"

I nodded. Even with my old astigmatic eyes I could see a strange crease down the middle of the man's scalp.

"Well, he's called 'The Miracle Man,' and he IS a Christian!"

I sat enraptured while the inmate explained how this man had accepted Jesus and was baptized under armed guard in the prison. Since his life had been turned completely around, he no longer needed the cigarettes the prison used for partial payment on work crews. One of the other inmates, not understanding the situation, wanted those cigarettes and felt strongly that he ought to have them. Grabbing one of those huge stirring paddles from the soup caldron in the kitchen, he waited for the newly baptized Christian as he came up the stairs into the mess hall. Without warning he struck the man with the sharp edge of the paddle, popping his skull as if it were a gourd. They rushed the poor man to the prison hospital, but his prognosis looked very bleak indeed.

"We all knew this guy was gonna check out," the inmate next to me explained. "That's when they called some of us together for a special prayer meetin'. Unless God did somethin', and did it fast, it would be all over for him. Well, miracle number one happened. He lived!"

"You say number one. What was number two?" I asked.

"Well, first ya gotta understand somethin' about prison life." It was then he ushered me into the violent, revengeful world behind bars, where the code is to retaliate. Men sometimes make long knives called "shives" in the machine shop and hide them in their trouser leg. When a guard isn't watching in the recreation yard, or "jungle," as it is called, a fellow inmate may drop in a pool of blood. Eyes turn the other direction. Nobody admits to having seen a thing. Or an inmate may wait at the top of the stairs, and to even a score he may trip a victim and send him to the hospital with a broken leg or worse. No witnesses testify; it was all "accidental."

"Well, when this black guy gets outta the hospital we expected him to go right back to the mess hall and get even with the guy who did the caper on him. In fact the kitchen guy was waitin' for him with his fists clenched at the top of the stairs where he had creased his skull. It was gonna be a fight for sure!

"But now comes miracle number two. Instead of fightin' him, the black guy comes on smilin'. He told him, 'Ya expect me to fight ya, don't ya? Well I'm notta gonna because I love Jesus, and that makes all the difference. I'm not mad at ya. I'm prayin' for ya.' "

The inmate next to me leaned closer. "Ya know, around here we rate a real Christian on the basis that he doesn't pay back. That's the test, mister!"

A text flashed through my mind. "And the work of righteousness shall be peace; and the effect of righteousness quietness and assurance for ever." Isaiah 32:17. The Miracle Man was a testimony of true sanctification.

The apostle John was like that. Of all the disciples he most fully reflected the character of Christ. When he first came to Jesus he was wrapped up in himself, combative, belligerent, critical, impetuous, self-assertive, and proud. John oozed with unlovely traits that hid much of his warm, positive side. He and his brother James didn't get their explosive handle, "Sons of Thunder," by accident. Yet we have no record of John's ever "trying" to die to self. That never works anyway; self has a way of crawling off the altar of sacrifice.

But John gave us the secret in his consistent proximity to Jesus. "As the character of the Divine One was manifested to him, he saw his own deficiency and was humbled by the knowledge. The strength and patience, the power and tenderness, the majesty and meekness, that he beheld in the daily life of the Son of God, filled his soul with admiration and love. Day by day his heart was drawn out toward Christ, until he lost sight of self in love for his Master."[6] The old John died. As he beheld a balanced Jesus and His perfect character and accepted of His enabling grace, his whole nature was transformed.

The man who once could easily fly into a rage wrote, "We know we have passed from death unto life, because we love the brethren." 1 John 3:4. The man who once asked permission to have a heavenly fire bomb destroy the Samaritans who had miffed him, could write, "If a man say, I love God, and hateth his brother, he is a liar." 1 John 4:20. The very man who once engaged in a heated debate over who was the greatest could pen, "Love not the world, neither the things that are in the world." 1 John 2:15. As self passed away John clearly awakened to the soft, subduing influence of Jesus. He never claimed to be sinless, but he did claim that a knowledge of God would fill the soul until there was no more clamoring of the carnal nature.

Ellen White says that "to give glory to God is to reveal His character in our own, and thus make Him known. And in whatever way we make known the Father or the Son, we glorify God."[7]

Is it any wonder that the angel shouted, "Give glory to him?"

---

1. *The Desire of Ages*, p. 36.
2. Ellen G. White, *Counsels on Diet and Foods,* p. 35.
3. Ellen G. White, *Evangelism*, pp. 271, 272.
4. *The Desire of Ages*, p. 330.
5. *Testimonies*, vol. 1, p. 131.
6. Ellen G. White, *Steps to Christ,* p. 73.
7. Ellen G. White Comments, *SDA Bible Commentary,* vol. 7, p. 979.

"The hour of his judgment is come." Revelation 14:7.

The Brink of Eternity

On that bitterly cold, star-studded night of April 14, 1912, the great White Star liner *Titanic* slid gracefully through the calm North Atlantic water. It was almost 11:40 p.m. Up ahead an iceberg loomed dangerously near. And then it happened. At the very last moment the ship veered to port, brushing the berg and leaving a 300-foot gash in her side. It seemed almost impossible that this massive ship, nearly three football fields long and declared by some to be unsinkable, should be mortally wounded. But she was! Her first five watertight compartments were hopelessly flooded. She could float with four of her 16 watertight compartments flooded, but no matter how many switches were pulled to slam the emergency doors she would ultimately go down. With five compartments flooded the great ship would sink steadily until each of the remaining compartments filled. There simply was no escape from the inevitable.

At 2:10 a.m. the staccato of the last wireless stuttered for help. Ten minutes later the moment of truth had arrived. The *Titanic* leaned sickeningly to port, slipped beneath the dark depths, and disappeared. It was like the death of a small town. Of the nearly 3,000 on board, only 705 survived in half-filled lifeboats.

Relentlessly and surely, another moment of truth will ultimately press upon all professed believers the thrust of those words, "The hour of his judgment is come." Spiritual procrastination may plague us, but the fact remains that the final investigation of our honest standing before God is now being checked. The exhausting, fast-clipped pace of our daily routine seldom provides an opportunity to pause and reflect on what is happening in Christ's closing work in the heavenly sanctuary. That seems too far removed from reality for many of us. Everything seems the same. There might be a slight list to this old planet, but the lights are still on, the band plays, and normalcy continues to be gauged by the all-pervasive mass media. A quick check of the evening news and, strangely enough, it reassures us in its own morbid way that all is the same. Crime, calamities, politics, sports, war, and weather laced with those commercials about headache remedies and other so-called human needs settle us into a sickening complacency.

Satan keeps inventing even greater schemes to keep our minds occupied. He is keenly aware of what happens here and in heaven. "He knows that with him *everything* depends on his diverting minds from Jesus and His truth."[1] The last thing he wants is for anyone to catch the satisfying peace and joy of knowing God intimately. So he has to be creative to turn our attention. If we are not preoccupied with the cares of this life, entertainment waits in the wings. And if sex, violence and vice do not captivate, he thrusts comedy at us. It works with many. Prayer and Bible study are about as flat and uninteresting as memorizing a large city phone directory after we have been saturated with feigned emotions and frivolity.

The fervor of our early preaching of the judgment-hour message has all been drowned out by the cacophony of current events. The consistency of contemporary crises creates an atmosphere of complacency that diverts attention from the real issue of personal preparation. It does seem hard to focus attention on the fact that above the turmoil on this planet God silently and patiently works out the counsels of His own will. But He really does! "Today men and nations are being measured by the plummet in the hand of Him who makes no mistake. All are by their own choice deciding their destiny, and God is overruling all for the accomplishment of His purposes."[2]

Faith had certainly grown dim for the Jewish people prior to Christ's first advent. The grinding oppression of the Roman government seemed to counter any claim that a Messiah was on His way. God's predictions had apparently died in a whimper amidst the clutches of a heathen rule. Yet "when the fulness of time was come, God sent forth his Son." Galatians 4:4.

God's timing is always razor sharp and marvelous to behold. Mary's pregnancy and trip to Bethlehem fit neatly into place, even though women were not required by law to appear for the census taking. Then suddenly, "when the great clock of time pointed to that hour, Jesus was born in Bethlehem."[3] That little obscure village manger became bright with the proof of God's special ability to bring to pass, right on schedule, that which seemed so impossible.

Those quiet years at Nazareth speak eloquently of God's purpose in allowing no haste and no delay. Jesus did not become restless during His teens. He kept on sawing and hammering and keeping pace with the local furniture orders through His nineteenth birthday. He didn't count the next decade as a waste of time either. He made each day count, and the things He built testified that what He was doing at that moment was a priority item.

Then one day word reached His little hill town that His cousin John, whom He had never seen, was baptizing down at the Jordan. The signal! Then and only then did Jesus close the carpenter shop. The phase of trade and tools, which had occupied so much of His time up to this point, was over. It was now the autumn of A.D. 27. Jesus could say with assurance, "The time is fulfilled." Mark 1:15.

When the hour finally arrived for Him to make His last journey to Jerusalem, "He set His face steadfastly to go to persecution, denial, rejection, condemnation, and death."[4] Jesus knew He was in the midst of the prophetic week of Daniel 9, and He died exactly on time!

When Stephen laid down his life as the first Christian martyr it signaled the end of the Jewish nation as God's representatives. From then on the gospel would go to the Gentiles, and all those who accepted Christ would be counted as "Abraham's seed, and heirs according to the promise." Galatians 3:29.

Still there remained 1,810 years before the judgment. Paul on Mars Hill urged the people to repent "because he hath appointed a day, in the which he will judge the world in righteousness." Acts 17:31. And when the apostle stood before Felix, "he reasoned of righteousness, temperance, and judgment to come." Acts 24:25. Felix trembled because the last thing he wanted to think about was a judgment. Yet it was a fact.

October 22, 1844, terminated the Bible's longest time prophecy and vaulted Jesus into the final phase of His work in the heavenly sanctuary. The antitypical Day of Atonement was not the return of Jesus, but a fulfillment of that ancient yearly drama that caused such heart searching among God's ancient Jewish people.

And herein lies the heart of the whole scheme. That annual symbolic ritual in the desert impressed upon the Israelites the truth about the holiness of God and His utter abhorrence of sin. But further it showed them "that they could not come in contact with sin without becoming polluted."[5]

Admittedly, contemporary living does not accommodate that ancient ritual very well. We may find the symbolism of candlesticks, incense, sacrificial offering, and scapegoat interesting adjuncts to our understanding of sacred history, yet the entire coverage seldom impresses us very deeply. We simply have a hard time visualizing it on a grand, heavenly scale, and we fail to catch the impact of our personal involvement. Perhaps we need to approach the whole investigative judgment from another direction.

It must be remembered that it is the hour of *God's* judgment. From a certain point of view He is on trial before His universe over the way He has conducted Himself in the great controversy with Satan. Accusations that His system of government, His law, His justice are faulty still thunder from the enemy camp. The exoneration of His people therefore vindicates His character. "The very image of God is to be reproduced in humanity. The honor of God, the honor of Christ, is involved in the perfection of the character of His people."[6] We become the witnesses at the very end of time that God's way of love actually works, even though Satan's forces are experienced in the subtle allurements of sin.

Through His Spirit we can be made fit to live with angels! And because of this we certainly are deeply involved in that final investigation of all those who have ever professed to serve Him. But more than this, the whole unfallen universe waits on tiptoe. The investigation is not conducted for the information of any member of the Deity, but for all those who know that they will one day have us as neighbors—the unfallen beings of the universe! God wants them to be satisfied that we are fit for heaven.

How well I remember the day I stood outside the prison psychiatrist's office in the criminally insane ward of a state penitentiary, waiting to see a man I had held Bible studies with for about a year. The doctor stepped into the hallway. He would not allow me to see the inmate right then because he was getting ready to leave for his final hearing before the judge. Harold had been in lock-up for nearly five years, and that was about the limit in that state. After that the inmates were considered "cured" and were released.

The psychiatrist looked intently into my eyes. "I've got a question for you, Mr. Doward. Would you want Harold living next door as a neighbor?"

Without hesitation I shook my head. No way would I want that man as a neighbor! This was no snap judgment. I knew him! Even though he had nearly finished the Bible studies and had talked of baptism, there remained a twist to his tormented mind that he had not allowed to be straightened out. He was unfit for society.

Earlier Harold had killed his girlfriend with a broken bottle. That was what had thrust him into prison in the first place. The memory of his prostitute mother forcing him to live in the back seat of an old car and find food for himself as a lad had produced spasms of hatred against all women.

Even while behind bars he once borrowed a female social worker's glasses and crushed them in his bare hands, symbolically saying to her how he really felt. He was a misogynist to the core!

Harold had answered an Adventist magazine ad for Bible studies, and that was where I entered the scene. I visited Harold weekly, and he seemed to make real progress in understanding the Scriptures. I could never see his face clearly because of the heavy wire mesh that separated us when we talked, but from his tone of voice and penetrating questions it all seemed so hopeful. Once, however, he asked if the Adventist Church had any women in it. I thought at the time that this was a strange question to ask, but failed to catch the significance because I did not then fully know about his background. I even brought my wife out for a visit and encouraged my secretary to enter the scene so he could meet Christian women.

But then things went haywire for Harold. He began writing bizarre letters to my secretary that were a mishmash of sexual fantasies strung together with the beasts of Daniel and Revelation. This occurred shortly before my final visit to the penetentiary and my meeting with the psychiatrist. Now I was informed that Harold might be released! I simply could not accept the notion that he should go free. In spite of all the state laws and massive paperwork, Harold remained a potentially very dangerous person.

Imagine how the angels must feel as they watch us in action! We claim to be scheduled for release from this earth, which in itself intensifies their interest. Will grasping covetousness emerge later in the Holy City as someone tries to chip away at the streets of gold? Will heaven's tranquillity suddenly be shattered by angry voices? Will someone seek to elbow his way forward to snatch away a supposedly higher position? Having seen what sin does, all heaven is determined that the great controversy shall not be recycled. There must never again enter the madness of selfishness. Therefore it is absolutely essential that God vindicate Himself in accepting some and rejecting others.

The unerring accuracy of the heavenly data processing is total and covers three areas. The book of life lists all who have ever entered the service of God. The book of remembrance contains all those words of faith and acts of love, for "in the book of God's remembrance every deed of righteousness is immortalized."[7] Finally, heaven retains a record of the sins of men which even covers the secret purposes and motives, penetrating every foggy maze men have contrived to cover their tracks. Unless repented of and forsaken, these sins will remain on file to stand witness against the sinner who refuses Christ's pardon and His blotting out from the record.

"Sin may be concealed, denied, covered up from father, mother, wife, children, and associates; no one but the guilty actors may cherish the least suspicion of the wrong; but it is laid bare before the intelligences of heaven."[8] Heaven places absolutely no value on profession. Only the motivation of love will count. A mere performance record for any other purpose will not stand the test. Those who have accumulated church activities as a cushion will receive a shocker when Jesus tells them flatly, "I never knew you!"

Satan is the ultimate legalist. He never misses an accusation. The enemy has an accurate printout of sins too. He knows the minute details of every successful temptation. He points with triumph to our record and exultingly says, "In all fairness, Lord, You cannot accept any of these who claim to be Your people. Are these the ones who are supposed to take my place and the place of my colleagues? Surely, Lord, this cannot be just. They have engaged in selfish activities, the very same kind that led You to ban us from heaven." And then with his record in hand he goes down the list of successful bids for his allegiance. No amount of good deeds can erase that kind of exposure. Since Satan is the "accuser of the brethren," none can escape his probing, accusing finger. We desperately need an advocate!

Enter Jesus! In the ancient symbolism He is both the Lamb and the High Priest. He retains the right to represent us because of His tremendous sacrifice. He is not interested in Satan's protracted checklist, nor is He impressed with the devil's diabolical ability to tap the weaknesses of humanity. But He is vitally interested in our response to His love. He will never turn away from the broken and contrite heart. Deep repentance and a forsaking of evil captivate His attention. He never argues with the accuser. He has something on hand that is not available to Satan. The limit of the enemy's accuracy is contained within an outward performance; the rest is surmising. Satan may impugn our best motives and question our sincerity, but Jesus holds a record of the heart! And since He has never lost a case, that good news ought to make us rejoice in this time of the investigative judgment.

Unwittingly we have sometimes projected the notion that God is out to get the sinner and that, if it were not for Jesus, he would succeed. Even little children unconsciously pick this up. A friend's precocious little daughter was startled late one afternoon when a sudden hailstorm burst violently upon their home. The hailstones rattled on the roof and nearly shattered the windows. Wide-eyed with fright, she ran to Daddy. "Who ordered that?" she pointed upward.

Her father chuckled and began teasing her a little about who possibly could have dumped such a flurry of ice from the skies, but she was serious. "I mean, it came from heaven, didn't it?" she asked.

"Well, that's true."

"Then God must have ordered it. Jesus wouldn't do such a thing!" she said emphatically.

Now my friend wasn't chuckling any more. He probed to find out just where his daughter had picked up such an idea. He discovered it came from Sabbath School, where she had been told of Jesus' pleading before the Father on our behalf.

I hope this childish distortion was erased, yet the image of Jesus doing His best to hold back the wrath of God does come through periodically. It sometimes unconsciously pervades even the preaching of pastors and evangelists. How tragic that people, and especially children, aren't told that "the Father himself loveth you." John 16:27. The topic of the investigative judgment lends itself to such a distortion unless properly understood and presented. We must never forget that "God was in Christ, reconciling the world unto himself." 2 Corinthians 5:19. It was God the Father who gave His only begotten Son that we might have life. Satan is still up to his old tricks of trying to shift the blame for his own tyrannical rule.

Humanity seems to enjoy anything that smacks of an anthropomorphic nature. Animal antics especially please us if in any way they resemble our behavior. But there is always a problem when this tendency splashes over into concepts of God and how He functions. And the investigative judgment sometimes seems to present strange mental pictures of God's calculations. For example, we know that names are accepted and names rejected and that the cases of the dead come first. But if God should go down some heavenly alphabetical list of the living as we probably would do, He might start with Anderson and go on through to Zimmerman. And if that were the case Zimmerman would apparently stand a better chance than Anderson. Then things get a bit sticky thinking about Anderson walking about with his case fixed for eternity prior to the close of probation. And what if Zimmerman dies suddenly in a flaming car wreck and is wiped off the living list? Now we are getting even stickier.

That is always the problem when we try to fit God into our practices and make Him in our own image. God does not do things that way. He is never caught off guard by sudden disasters or changes of events. There are no emergencies with Him. He can produce an instant replay of any professed believer, twenty-four hours a day. "God judges every man according to his work. Not only does He judge, but He sums up, day by day and hour by hour, our progress in well-doing."[9]

We are on the brink of eternity. It is like the two-minute warning of a football game. The end-time game plan shifts then. Everything is played differently when that warning is given. What might have been acceptable earlier no longer applies. Unconsciously the whole world is maneuvering into place for a final stand of loyalty or disloyalty to God.

When Christ returns the second time those who do not *reflect* His image fully will be destroyed by the brightness of His coming. If sin, unconfessed and unrepented of, remains a part of the life, you will be consumed by the destroying presence of Him whose brightness is like a devouring fire. "While the investigative judgment is going forward in heaven, while the sins of penitent believers are being removed from the sanctuary, there is to be a special work of purification, of putting away of sin, among God's people upon earth."[10]

We desperately need to stop being critical of each other and be very critical of ourselves. Our own thoughts and actions need to come under careful scrutiny. "Examine yourselves. . . . Do you not realize that Christ Jesus is in you—unless, of course, you fail the test?" 2 Corinthians 13:5, NIV.

While a permissive society shouts, "Express yourself!" Christ says, "Control yourself by the grace I offer you." Those carnal imaginations, stimulated by every mass media device available to deprave humanity, must be turned over to Christ, who can keep us from sinning. It will do no good to set up our own criteria for right and wrong. God's great law is the standard in the judgment, and Christ has made ample provision to meet the claims of that law. Anyone who mutters, "I can't make it, so why try?" is only echoing a devilish lie. If we are lost the only reason will be that we did not choose to be saved.

Heaven's judgment hour announcement is not designed to frighten but to bring preparation and hope. Those who have learned to love and fear God in the right sense will rest their cases with the One who came to save them. The close of probation on this planet means rescue is on the way! And that presents an urgency to our lives in personal commitment to Christ and making plain the principles at stake in the great controversy to all who will give heed.

On May 7, 1942, two fleets engaged in a battle without a

single surface ship firing a shot. It was a first in naval history and became known as the Battle of the Coral Sea. As the battle raged between the carrier fleets, a thrilling incident developed in the near sunset of the trying day of fighting.

Paul Baker, flying back to the aircraft carrier *Lexington* after an engagement with the Japanese, heard a terse command over his radio, "Extinguish your landing lights. Enemy aircraft still present."

As Baker flipped the switch he spotted a Japanese plane out his port side. He turned to starboard and there was another. In all, ten zeros suddenly had boxed Baker in above, below, and on both sides. They had no intention of shooting him down; this American would lead them to a really worthwhile target.

Baker had only a moment to decide. He could fly back to the aircraft carrier and have the enemy planes crash dive into the *Lexington,* killing many of his comrades, or he could take the Japanese with him to his own death.

The officers on the bridge fairly held their breaths as they watched through binoculars the youngster turn his plane sharply and head for open sea in the gathering twilight. Even though the *Lexington* suffered such severe damage that it had to be sunk on the second day of fighting, it takes none of the luster away from Paul Baker's decision.

Sensing the urgency of the hour, can you make a decision and stick with it? There is no time to waste in contemplating the advantages of sin. A decision to bring full daily commitment to Christ must be made for time and eternity, for the hour of His judgment is come.

---

1. Ellen G. White, *The Great Controversy,* p. 488.
2. Ellen G. White, *Education,* p. 178.
3. *The Desire of Ages,* p. 32.
4. *The Desire of Ages,* p. 486.
5. *The Great Controversy,* p. 419.
6. *The Desire of Ages,* p. 671.
7. *The Great Controversy*, p. 481.
8. *Ibid.,* p. 486.
9. Ellen G. White Comments, *SDA Bible Commentary,* vol. 7, p. 987.
10. *The Great Controversy,* p. 425.

"Worship him that made heaven, and earth, and the sea, and the fountains of waters." Revelation 14:7.

Lift Up Your Eyes

Man has a basic need to worship. He inevitably will find something—the sun, rivers, snakes, the dead—just about anything that his local culture and tradition has encouraged, and make a god out of it.

Several years ago while visiting the Far East, I watched with fascination as a young woman continually threw down her charm blocks within a Buddhist shrine. The blocks resembled huge dice, and when these were lined up with the right combination of characters printed on the top, they were supposed to bring good luck. Repeatedly she bounced the blocks on the floor until finally the characters were aligned perfectly. Her face lit up and, bringing her hands together in prayer, she bowed her head reverently toward the large idol and left. I wondered what inner peace and satisfaction she found in those charm blocks. It was obvious to me that she had been worshiping something.

But God's claim to reverence and worship above all the gods known to the heathen world rests solidly upon the fact that He alone is Creator and that to Him all beings owe their existence. The first angel's message concludes with an appeal to worship Him who created all things.

The psalmist opens to us God's creative genius by announcing, "All the gods of the nations are idols: but the Lord made the heavens." Psalm 96:5. And those very heavens "declare the glory of God." Psalm 19:1. The Lord through the prophet Isaiah asks, "To whom then will ye liken me, or shall I be equal? saith the Holy One. Lift up your eyes on high, and behold who hath created these things." Isaiah 40:25, 26.

From the twinkling stars and systems and swirling galaxies we realize only a tiny fraction of the greatness of our God. The mind fairly reels with the staggering reality of the infinitude of space. Whatever earthbound bigness impresses humanity is instantly swallowed up in the utter vastness of the universe.

Knowing that astronomers use the light unit for measuring distances beyond our solar system intrigued me in my younger days. I used to go out at night and shine a flashlight heavenward, intently watching to see if I could possibly catch the movement of that beam traveling at 186,000 miles a second. Of course anything that can zip along so fast as to be able to belt the equator seven-and-a-half times in a second, or travel to the moon in a little more than a second certainly would seem instantaneous At that speed light races along at more than 11 million miles a minute and travels more than 16 billion miles a day. Multiply that by 365 days and you have one light year, or nearly 6 trillion miles. But one light year is a short hop in space. The nearest star to our solar system, Alpha Centauri, is 4.25 light years away!

Looking at the beautiful photographs taken through the Hale telescope on Mount Palomar only hints at the enormous caverns of the universe. Our imagination is stretched to the limit as we try to visualize light speeding along through interstellar space, down the vast corridors of time millions of years before our earth came into existence, and finally striking the sensitive film of a photographic plate. The best modern telescopes reach about 500 million light years, yet there remains an infinity beyond.

Our solar system with its nine orbiting planets is tucked away off in one corner of our Milky Way Galaxy. Our earth-level, edgewise view of this galaxy does not permit an adequate concept of its vastness, but if we were to see it all from far off in space and at another angle, the Milky Way would appear as a giant spiral, 100,000 light years across.

Our sun would be only a pinpoint of light, nearly lost amidst the estimated 100 billion other stars in our galactic system. But backing off far enough, the whole Milky Way Galaxy would appear as only another twinkling star in the heavens. Imagine it, one galaxy! "Telescopes on Mt. Palomar can see as many as a million galaxies inside the bowl of the Big Dipper alone."[1] The Scriptures have reason to declare, "These are but the outer fringe of his works; how faint the whisper we hear of him! Who then can understand the thunder of his power?" Job 26:14, NIV.

The immensity of time and space are incomprehensible to finite minds. God's eternity can be dimly contemplated by beholding the present, but eternity stretching endlessly in both directions is beyond our understanding! Someone has expressed this thought in these words:

"God called up from dreams a man into the vestibule of heaven, saying, 'Come thou hither, and see the glory of My house.' And to the servants that stood around His throne He said, 'Take him, and undress him from his robes of flesh; cleanse his vision and put a new breath into his nostrils: only touch not with any change his human heart,—the heart that weeps and trembles.' It was done: and with a mighty angel for his guide, the man stood ready for his infinite voyage; and from the terraces of heaven, without sound of farewell, at once they wheeled into endless space. . . .

"Then from a distance that is counted only in heaven, light dawned for a time through a sleepy film; by unutterable space the light swept to them, they by unutterable space to the light. In a moment, the blazing of suns was around them.

"Then came eternities of twilight, that revealed, but were not revealed. On the right hand and on the left towered mighty constellations . . . that seemed ghostly from infinitude. Without measure were the architraves, past numbers were the archways, beyond memory the gates. Within were stars that scaled eternities below; above was below, below was above to the man stripped of gravitating body. Depth was swallowed up in height insurmountable; height was swallowed up in depth unfathomable. Suddenly as thus they tilted over abysmal worlds,—a mighty cry arose,—that systems more mysterious, that worlds more billowy, other heights and other depths, were coming, were nearing, were at hand.

"Then the man sighed, and stopped, shuddered, and wept. His overladen heart uttered itself in tears, and he said: 'Angel, I will go no farther; for the spirit of man acheth with this infinity. Insufferable is the glory of God. Let me lie down in the grave, and hide me from the persecution of the infinite; for end, I see, there is none.' And from the listening stars that shone around issued a choral voice: 'The man speaks truly: end there is none that ever yet we heard of.' 'End is there none?' the angel solemnly demanded; 'Is there no end? And this is the sorrow that kills you?' But no voice answered, that he might answer himself. Then the angel threw up his glorious hands to the heavens, saying: 'End there is none to the universe of God. Lo, also, there is no beginning!' "[2]

When Christ met Moses at the burning bush He identified Himself as "I AM that I AM." He who was the I AM from eternity in the past, that I AM of the present, is also the I AM of the future. In His classic confrontation with the Jews, Jesus declared, "Before Abraham was, I AM." John 8:58. Silence settled over those bigoted leaders. That Jesus should take the title of deity upon His lips seemed to them an intolerable, blasphemous claim. They reached down to take up stones to kill Him. Yet the very Man who stood before them that day was actually from eternity!

The striking orderliness of the universe should give rise to a greater sense of awe and profound worship. From the tiniest atom to the greatest star, all have orbital patterns. When Ellen White declares that the redeemed "with undimmed vision . . . gaze upon the glory of creation—suns and stars and systems, all in their appointed order circling the throne of Deity," she is expressing a profound truth, even though it is stated in almost poetic language.[3]

A cosmic view from the minutest to the greatest invariably enhances worship. The thought that God is in touch with all His vast creation produces profound trust. "He telleth the number of the stars; he calleth them all by their names. Great is our Lord, and of great power: his understanding is infinite." Psalm 147:4, 5. Not only does He have every star numbered and named, but He is fully aware of the little brown sparrow and the crustacean on the seashore. Whenever we are prone to feel lonely, remember His omnipresence. Pulse beat follows pulse beat because His power is there!

When you feel discouraged or depressed, go walk among the stars. Imagine this world as a giant glass ball where you could see stars below you and to the sides as well as above. Then visualize His power to create all this.

Watching the reverse action of a motion picture taken during an explosion of some structure is fascinating. The dust particles and pieces come together in a grand fashion to form the object. But think of the psalmist's words, "By the word of the Lord were the heavens made; and all the host of them by the breath of his mouth." "For he spake, and it was done; he commanded, and it stood fast." Psalm 33:6, 9. Crystalized energy! And that same power to create suns and systems, and the atom, can transform a tangled life and bring order out of chaos, remaking you and me into His own image, and bringing hope and joy and peace in the process.

Eternity will not be sufficient to comprehend the full measure of God's wonders. But we must start here to develop thinking habits that will lift our eyes to greater appreciation of our God. Think, for example, of just one aspect of the natural world, bird migration. Year after year birds follow trackless skyways around the globe. In their tiny brains God has placed incredible skills and navigational aids.

Many astonishing feats of bird migration could be recited, but one stands out among the rest. Several years ago a female bobolink was captured near Kenmare, North Dakota, and shipped to Dr. William J. Hamilton, III, of the California Academy of Sciences in Berkeley. When she arrived by air that late summer Dr. Hamilton banded the little bird, but soon after she escaped. Months slipped by, and the next spring Dr. Hamilton received a phone call from Kenmare with the exciting news that the same bobolink with the colored rings around her legs was back. The mystery deepens here because western bobolinks do not stay in the United States during winter but often migrate as far south as Brazil. And Berkeley is certainly not on any migratory path for bobolinks. "Somehow the bird was able to compensate for her displacement by airplane from North Dakota, make her way to the wintering ground, and return to her previous home by solving a problem of difficulty even for a human with navigator's instruments."[4]

Scientists now know that birds use a complex combination of sensory data that range from the sun, air masses, humidity, and even radio waves to guide them across trackless oceans and vast land masses. Long before the present scientific data was available William Cullen Bryant caught the spiritual overtones of that Power that guides birds along ancient flyways, when he wrote "To a Waterfowl." His closing lines have a direct appeal to our trust in God:

> He who from zone to zone
> Guides through the boundless sky thy certain flight,
> In the long way that I must tread alone
> Will guide my steps aright.

Wherever we look in the natural world there are marvels and challenging mysteries that point unmistakably to a divine Planner. Nature itself speaks to our sense of design and forethought. A God who enjoys such variety and multitude of wonders and beauty is worthy of our worship. The weekly Sabbath celebration of creation is designed to enhance such worship. This fact sets the stage for the enemy's final end-time counter move.

The centuries faded away without the slightest hint of any evolutionary theory being promulgated. Interestingly enough it was after the first angel's message began to sound that Charles Darwin published his famous *On the Origin of Species* in 1859. While a few men had explored such notions prior to this time, it wasn't until then that the idea really captivated men's imaginations. Today we are immersed in this myth. Dr. Clark H. Pinnock has captured this idea well in his book *Set Forth Your Case*.

"Every generation has its myths, and it is always easier to detect the myths of other cultures than our own. A myth is a story which offers an imaginary explanation for the origin and shape of life. So pervasively does it envelop the culture, and so exactly does it coincide with the contemporary spirit, that its inner absurdities go almost unnoticed. Anyone who would dare to dispute it is considered foolish. All educated people in the twelfth century knew the earth was flat. No other possibility was even considered. *Evolution* is the cultural myth of the twentieth century. It offers to provide a total explanation of all reality without requiring man to answer to the God of creation. It is religious to the core. . . .

"Almost every generation of men have believed themselves to be at the apex of knowledge. This makes the myths especially difficult to expose. Scientifically the concept of evolution has almost outworn its usefulness. So many inner contradictions have been pointed out that the hypothesis has ceased to be helpful. Yet the brainwashing goes on. High school textbooks, educational TV science programs, and the popular press continue to play on men's gullibility. Evolution (as if the term conveys a precise entity) is presentated 'as it happened.' Charts illustrating life's progress over millions of years are shown. It would almost lead one to believe the magazine had live coverage! All this despite the admitted fact that no scientist has come anywhere near demonstrating an unbroken line of evolution with any certainty. It is totally irresponsible to give the impression to students that evolution (whatever that means) is a demonstrated fact, or even a secure hypothesis. One can only conclude that the ruling intelligentsia have some motive for pushing this myth and converting people to it. The motive is not difficult to discern. For the myth allows secular man to retain his autonomy without losing his freedom, or so they hope, . . . for a mechanical nature which runs on the lines of physical causation cannot easily become the mother of free and significant human beings. The two motifs clash with one another in a new form of the age-old paradox between freedom and determinism. But modern man needs his myth badly. Nature is his mother and her laws his principles, because he will not have God to reign over him. Yet freedom is his hope because otherwise he is a machine too. And so he is caught between two total and contradictory claims. Yet he prefers this tension to acknowledging the rights of the King.

"Evolution succeeds not because it is a sound theory, but because it bolsters the humanistic faith which modern man has foolishly adopted in place of the Christian gospel. It persists despite nature, not because of her. . . .

"Every theory so far requires a miracle somewhere along the way greater than creation itself."[5]

When my wife and I took in the latest scientific film explanation of creation at the Reuben H. Fleet Space Theater in San Diego, we were greeted with such an astounding demand for faith that it left us stunned. The narrator first intoned, "You see 5 billion years compressed into 30 seconds as you watch a galaxy form." And from then on everything was compressed, including the creation of life on this planet. The screen was nearly dark except for a few highlighted glimpses of ocean waves. Then suddenly the screen was "shattered" by a bolt of lightning. The sound of thunder rocked the theater. The narrator informed us that when the lightning struck the water, life was formed. A small wiggler—some unidentified lower form of life—began to emerge from the primordial soup, and crawled up on land, where in that same compressed time mode it inexplicably developed legs and eventually stood upright and became a man before our eyes! I leaned over and whispered to my wife, "That certainly takes a lot of faith to believe!" And yet evolutionary scientists reject creationism out of hand because it strays, according to their concepts, into the non-scientific field of faith!

Evolution's intransigence is not without its tragic overtones. The concept, tenaciously holding that all creation emerged from blind chance, turns the source of all reality into chaos. This persistent theme of lawlessness and the survival-of-the-fittest motif has invaded every aspect of modern society, filtering right down to the wild expressions of modern art and music. But worse, it has robbed man of his high destiny and negated his need for a Saviour.

"Men are so intent upon excluding God from the sovereignty of the universe that they degrade man and defraud him of the dignity of his origin. . . . The genealogy of our race, as given by inspiration, traces back its origin, not to a line of developing germs, mollusks, and quadrupeds, but to the great Creator. Though formed from the dust, Adam was 'the son of God.' "[6]

A few years ago a psychologist friend of mine attended a national convention for those schooled in this discipline. During a discussion period, he asked: "If the evolutionary theory is built upon a need, how do you explain why millions of human brain cells serve no function?"

All eyes turned toward my friend. "How do *you* explain it?" they demanded.

My friend smiled. "Man was made in the image of God and built for eternity!"

The first angel's message will continue to sound to the end of time. It prepares men to receive the other angel voices from the sky. We desperately need right now to know the full meaning of worship. The Sabbath itself is tightly bound up with this message. Our concept of God and His day of rest will help us stand unmoved during the final crisis.

Right after World War II, I heard a missionary tell of his attempt to translate the Bible into the Tibetan language. When he came to the opening phrase "In the beginning God," his native translator stopped. "Which god do you want here? The god of the rocks, the mountains, the streams? Which one?"

"I want the God who created them all. The God of creation!" the missionary replied.

"We have no word for that."

"Then we shall make one."

And the newly coined word for God with a capital letter came into being. This was the God who could really be worshiped because He "made heaven, and earth, and the sea, and the fountains of waters."

1. *The National Geographic*, May 1974, p. 592.

2. Lucas A. Reed, *Astronomy and the Bible*, (Pacific Press Publishing Association, 1919), pp. 119-121.

3. *The Great Controversy,* pp. 677, 678.

4. "Marvels and Mysteries of Our Animal World," *Readers' Digest,* 1964.

5. Charles H. Pinnock, *Set Forth Your Case* (Nutley, New Jersey: The Craig Press, 1968), pp. 80, 81.

6. *Patriarchs and Prophets*, p. 45.

"Babylon is fallen, is fallen, that great city, because she made all nations drink of the wine of the wrath of her fornication." Revelation 14:8.

The System of Sin

Motivated by pride, the construction of the tower of Babel on the plain of Shinar projected disbelief in the true God. Rainbows are for believing, but the dwellers of Shinar chose to disbelieve God's promised sign never again to send another global deluge. In defiance of His will men built their monument to apostasy, the Tower of Babel, hoping to reach up to the heavens. After God scattered the builders, the grand citadel of rebellion crumbled into dust, yet there were those who later determined to choose the site for a city.

Outside the Genesis record Babel is called Babylon. Babel, synonymous with confusion, apparently did not appeal to the Babylonians who gave it the meaning of "the gate of the gods." In spite of this lofty pagan explanation, in the Bible Babylon ever retained its original symbolic concept of rebellion against the God of heaven and its resultant confusion.

The prophet Isaiah identifies Lucifer as the invisible king of Babylon. It was Satan's purpose to make Babylon the headquarters through which he intended to secure ultimate control of the human race. When Nebuchadnezzar rebuilt Babylon with its hanging gardens—one of the seven wonders of the ancient world—it was his desire to make his kingdom both universal and eternal. But Babylon fell, as God predicted it would, and Satan was forced to adjust his plans. The enemy tried through one world power after another to accomplish his ends, and might have succeeded had it not been for divine intervention.

By the end of the first century A.D. Christians sometimes cryptically referred to Rome as Babylon. Whether pagan or papal, literal or mystical, Babylon has been recognized down through the centuries as the traditional enemy of God's truth and His people.

While Satan worked through the various world powers that followed Babylon, his most audacious attempt to control the human race came through his masterpiece of deception, the papacy. This form of baptized paganism, utilizing the power of the state, attempted to compel men to obey its dictates as no power had heretofore attempted to do.

We must never lose sight of the picture of the overall struggle between the forces of good and evil on this planet. I remember once seeing a documentary film about an old cobbler at work. Outside of the opening sequence of the cobbler entering his shop, the rest was nothing more than a series of extreme close-ups of his hands, tacks, hammer-head, leather, stitches, glue, and all that goes on with shoe repair. The film never gained much prominence because of the consistent audience reaction to the suffocating oppression of the forced observation of the details. There was a screaming demand to back off and get an establishing shot, some wide-angle view that would capture the whole. In that revealing and strikingly current chapter "Liberty of Conscience Threatened" in the book *The Great Controversy*, we are furnished with a crisp establishing view of the long-standing conflict. "It is Satan's constant effort to misrepresent the character of God, the nature of sin, and the real issues at stake."[1]

We do not condemn the communicants of this religious system, many of whom are doubtless sincere. But the emergence of the papal system was no accident, and this is what the Scriptures condemn. It took time for Satan to develop this apostate church. His diabolical intention was to develop a religious system that would hold the widest possible appeal for humanity. The papacy "is prepared for two classes of mankind, embracing nearly the whole world— those who would be saved by their merits, and those who would be saved in their sins. Here is the secret of its power."[2]

By corrupting the pure truths of God's Word, Satan could effectively use this apostate church to blanket the nations with false doctrines and pleasing fables. Every heresy ultimately would distort the character of God in some fashion, lessen the obligations of God's law, and keep the true issues of the great controversy out of sight. Even a brief list of the papacy's falsehoods is revealing in the light of Christ's desire for His true church.

Tradition is used as a standard instead of the Word of God.

The doctrine of the immaculate conception claims that Mary the mother of Jesus was born sinless and thus denies that Christ shared our humanity.

The mediation of Christ in heaven has been set aside and replaced by an earthly priesthood.

Confession to a mere mortal separates the sinner from Christ, the only one who can forgive sins, and it elevates mere mortals to the place of God.

Salvation by works is substituted for salvation by faith.

The blasphemous doctrine of transubstantiation, by which the priest pretends to create the Creator in the idolatrous sacrifice of the mass, blurs the real meaning of communion.

The doctrine of the natural immortality of the soul removes the need for the resurrection and paves the way for spiritism. Out of this one falsehood alone has emerged saint worship, Mariolatry, purgatory, reward at death, and eternal torment.

Baptism by immersion, the symbol of Christ's death, burial, and resurrection, has been substituted by sprinkling and prepared the way for Sunday as the memorial of Christ's resurrection.

Sunday, borrowed from paganism, replaces the Sabbath, which God designed to remind man that He is the Creator and Saviour.

The doctrine of a temporal millennium, with a thousand

years of peace and prosperity, clears the way for Satan to impersonate Christ and cause the world to think that the long-expected millennium has arrived.

And what more could be said of papal infallibility and absolutism of the pope as the so-called vicar of Christ? The whole system fairly oozes with the foul corruption of nearly every true but perverted doctrine of God's Word. No wonder John was so entranced as he beheld Christ's revelation of this corrupt system, symbolized by an immoral woman riding a scarlet-colored beast, wearing on her forehead the designation: "MYSTERY, BABYLON THE GREAT, THE MOTHER OF HARLOTS AND ABOMINATIONS OF THE EARTH." Revelation 17:5.

In the closing verses of the first epistle of Peter appear these words, "The church which is at Babylon . . . greets you." Interestingly enough a footnote in a version of the Bible carrying the imprimatur of the papal church reads: "*Babylon:* Rome. A metaphor probably founded on Jewish usage." 1 Peter 5:13, Confraternity. So the identity of this religious system is clear. It is a religious system having its headquarters in Rome.

John the Revelator saw this religious system, symbolized by the fallen woman, using the state, represented by a seven-headed beast that conveyed her, drinking herself drunk with the blood of saints and martyrs. The prophet had no idea when he wrote this of the magnitude of the horrors that would be perpetrated by this religious system during the Dark Ages.

Christopher Wordsworth captured the horror well, when he wrote, "Heathen Rome doing the work of heathenism in persecuting the Church was *not* Mystery. But a *Christian Church*, calling herself the Mother of Christendom, and yet *drunken with the blood of saints*—this *is a Mystery*. A *Christian Church* boasting herself to be the Bride, and *being* the Harlot; styling herself Sion, and being Babylon—this *is* a *Mystery*. A *Mystery* indeed it is, that, when she says to all, 'Come unto me,' the voice from *heaven* should cry, '*Come out of her, My People*.' A *Mystery* indeed it is, that she who boasts herself the city of the Saints, should become *the habitation of devils*: that she who claims to be Infallible should be said to *corrupt the earth*: that a self-named *'Mother of Churches*,' should be called by the Holy Spirit the *'Mother of Abominations*:' that she who boasts to be Indefectible, should in one day be destroyed, and that Apostles should rejoice at her fall: that she who holds, as she says, in her hands the Keys of Heaven, should be cast into the lake of fire by Him Who has the Keys of hell. All this, in truth, *is* a great Mystery."[3]

But the expression "Babylon is fallen" applies more specifically to the condition of Protestantism. Paganism has been corrupt from its very beginning; at the time of the Protestant Reformation the papacy had been in a fallen condition for centuries; but during the Reformation of the sixteenth century, Protestants began to break away from papal domination and start a great work in returning to the primitive purity of the Christian faith, yet failed to keep moving upward. It was Protestantism, therefore, that was in a position to fall when the message of Revelation 14:8 began to sound in 1843.

"Babylon is said to be 'the *mother of harlots*.' By her *daughters* must be symbolized churches that cling to her doctrines and traditions, and follow her example of sacrificing the truth and the approval of God, in order to form an unlawful alliance with the world."[4] Most appropriately the term "Babylon" describes the confused condition of Protestants who claim the Bible as the basis of their existence yet who are divided into innumerable denominations, offshoots, and sects with conflicting theories and notions about what is truth.

When I first learned of the second angel's message it struck me with such a tremendous force that the impact is still with me. As I mentioned earlier, I had grown up in a large, mainline Protestant church steeped in liberal theology which interprets the Scriptures according to the dictates of self. While professing to base their faith on the the Bible, they in fact destroy its effectiveness by rejecting its authority. Liberal theology, as might be expected, excludes miracles—Christ didn't actually walk on the water, He only appeared to do so—the disciples were huddled so low in the boat that Jesus seemed to be walking on the water as He strolled along the shore!

In that very church the youth pastor, I later learned, dramatized the departure of that church from the true faith. One Sunday morning he brought a Bible to class to use as a visual aid. Instead of expounding the word of God from it, he explained to the young people that the Scriptures were nothing more than a collection of Hebrew myths and fairy tales. Then as he read selected passages from Genesis, he sneeringly tore out the pages, crumpled them up, and threw the wad in a corner. Steadily progressing through the Bible, he repeated his performance of disdain for the miracle records in the Word as far beneath the superior thinking of this enlightened age.

Finally there was nothing left but the covers, and with a grand demonstration of relief from the burden of the Book, he tossed these into the corner with an air of triumph, exclaiming, "And that's what we think of the Bible!" One young teenage girl fled sobbing from the room, shattered by the Sunday School lesson. Yet what could be expected from the youth pastor when his seminary training sent him down the long twilight road of humanism? Liberal theology early bought the evolutionary theory. The youth pastor's schooling only amplified the chance condition of man and left him dangling in infidelity in the name of Christianity.

The sure result of such theology is a surge toward the social gospel, which seeks to alter obvious community and social blights through legislation or whatever means are available rather than bring to people the truth of how Jesus Christ can transform individual lives.

In my teens one of the great issues at stake was how the local congregation could best work with the city government in cleaning up the red light district! This eloquent minister with an impressive disarranged alphabet after his name was always charmingly articulate and witty in public. People thronged to hear this "great doctor" on Sunday mornings. Undeniably he lived up to the performance challenge of his top salary. Very important people regularly joined the church. Such enrollment was viewed as being convenient and expedient because it extended respectability and confidence within the local community. But never was one word preached against the prevailing personal vices and sins which so effectively neutralize the real gospel. As a youngster I was shocked one Sunday morning when a deacon slipped out the side door of the church to sneak a quick smoke before serving communion. And yet, I felt little or no need for a crackdown on prostitution in town.

Ellen White describes such profession of religion well, when she says: "A high salary is paid for a talented minister to entertain and attract the people. His sermons must not touch popular sins, but be made smooth and pleasing for fashionable ears. Thus fashionable sinners are enrolled on the church records, and fashionable sins are concealed under a pretense of godliness."[5]

Whether liberal or conservative, both wings of apostate Protestantism cling tenaciously to a double falsehood inherited from Catholicism, which will eventually bring us to the final crisis. "Through the two great errors, the immortality of the soul and Sunday sacredness, Satan will bring the people under his deceptions. While the former lays the foundation of spiritualism, the latter creates a bond of sympathy with Rome. The Protestants of the United States will be foremost in stretching their hands across the gulf to grasp the hand of spiritualism; they will reach over the abyss to clasp hands with the Roman power; and under the influence of this threefold union, this country will follow in the steps of Rome in trampling on the rights of conscience."[6] We may have known these things for many years, yet the fulfillment of this last-day montage is developing right before our eyes!

Both the first and third angels give their messages in a "loud voice." The second simply makes the announcement of the fall of Babylon, and when the angel of Revelation 18 joins in the final call, it is written, "He cried mightily with a strong voice, saying, Babylon is fallen, is fallen." Revelation 18:2. The forceful repetition of the second angel's message is heaven's last best effort to arrest the attention of professed Christian churches to the seriousness of the situation within their ranks. This message is urgent! This angel amplifies the fallen state of Babylon in dramatic language by describing the hateful traits that heaven catalogues against apostate Christian bodies. It was after this that John heard another voice from heaven saying, "Come out of her, my people." Revelation 18:4.

It is not my purpose to condemn those who are in Babylon, but to *invite* them! The invitation is to join those who have taken their stand on the side of loyalty against every evil device with which the enemy intends to smear the good character of God. This is the Elijah message anew. In Elijah's day the people had unconsciously strayed into serving Baal. This Canaanite name means "lord." However, this was not the Lord of heaven. Baal was a god of human devising, one that satisfied the clamorings of the carnal nature. Fascinated by the hocus-pocus of the mystic rites, the people drifted farther and farther from the true God. Elijah's message was intended to snap them out of their deepening apostasy.

In our day some things have changed. People in developed countries seldom worship gods made from wood and stone. Yet it is quite easy to make a god out of false doctrines or theories which conceive of the living God in a wrong way. "Though in a different form, idolatry exists in the Christian world today as verily as it existed among ancient Israel in the days of Elijah."[7]

Seventh-day Adventists desperately need to understand their real mission and standing right now. In spite of voices to the contrary, we remain the only people on the face of the globe who can be identified as being the remnant church, designed by God to turn minds back to the true God. Such turning back inevitably enhances the quality of life and prepares people for the second advent. The very foundation of our faith rests in the proclamation of the truth about God's character which has been misunderstood and misinterpreted.

Tucked off in the last portion of that marvelously enlightening book *Christ's Object Lessons* is a statement that crystalizes the purpose of our existence. "The last rays of merciful light, the last message of mercy to be given to the world, is a revelation of His [God's] character of love."[8] Yet that concept has largely eluded us. Caught up in a Laodicean ego-inflating drive to proclaim our own good deeds, we have often been guilty of thwarting the very purpose of our existence. The good news is NOT about us!

Jesus came to correct the dark distortion circulating about a loving heavenly Father. Our own task is linked to His. Amidst all the contemporary misapprehensions and misunderstandings about a gracious God and the transcript of His character in His law, we seem bent on telling the world through every media possible what we have accomplished by our means and methods. But men seldom discover the real truth about God's character through some sort of osmosis of religious activity. The impact of our real message is too often lost amidst all the arm-waving gooddeed pictorials. After seeing one of our expensive national magazine ads, one man confided, "Adventists seem like nothing more than a glorified Red Cross."

Imagine the refreshing and salutary impact of some eye-catching advertisement or fair booth, designed to arrest the attention of even the most casual, to stop and consider that not every disaster or calamity is an "act of God." The great controversy motif impresses the mind with the reality of what is going on amidst all the turmoil and disorder on this planet. We of all people are able to present the depth of the meaning of the cross of Christ. In the glaring light of Golgotha, God's love is set in stark contrast with Satan's dark lies and exposes the enemy for the errors he has foisted upon humanity.

Our evangelistic outreach must never be satisfied by simply furnishing the public with bits and pieces of doctrinal truths. Two-by-fours and planks are "truths" of a building, but they certainly do not represent the finished construction. The doctrines have a place in fitting firmly together a framework of a total building about God's character. But if baptisms are based solely on a nodding consent to the fragments of truths, the real message of God's character and how it applies to daily living escapes the convert, and the end result often takes tragic turns. We must do more than prove to people that we can count to seven!

While we must ever carry the message with courtesy and tact, we must never flinch in exposing error. The call out of Babylon requires this. Jesus exerted a cutting edge during His confrontations with the religionists of His day. Without hesitation He laid bare their sins in a language which could not be misunderstood.

In this world truth will ever be on the scaffold, wrong forever on the throne. We were never commissioned to carry a popular message. But danger looms. Yielding to the inborn love of approbation invariably creates a penchant for some popular public relations image. It produces Aarons. "Woe unto you, when all men shall speak well of you!" Luke 6:26.

Any unrestrained desire by Seventh-day Adventists to be accepted in the Christian community inevitably ignores the danger of diluting our message and forges ahead with programs and preaching based on the watered-down message.

Remember, it is American apostate Protestantism that extends its hand across the gulf and clasps hands with spiritualism. As long as we relegate spiritualism to the seance room, the crystal ball, or Ouija board we shall never understand why the ultimate embrace takes place. We seem to forget the chameleonlike character of spiritualism. It knows just how to interpret the Bible to please the unrenewed heart and cover up vital truths. In a climate where Christian terminology such as "born again" or "the love of Jesus" is loosely used to carry on the most glaring departures from the real faith, spiritualism has a special knack for making Protestants feel comfortable. "*Love* is dwelt upon as the chief attribute of God, but it is degraded to a weak sentimentalism, making little distinction between good and evil.

God's justice, His denunciations of sin, the requirements of His holy law, are all kept out of sight."[9] This is one reason we should carefully scrutinize any efforts to adapt Babylon's methods to our message.

When Protestantism and spiritualism team up with Roman Catholicism in an unholy coalition using the state to crush any opposition to their religious zeal, we may be sure that all talk of human rights will vanish like so many soap bubbles in a high wind.

A bit of Babylon lies dormant in each of us. Self-seeking under the guise of godliness ever lurks in the shadows, and unless we are daily advancing in the Christian growth under the enabling power of God's Spirit we shall succumb to the popular demands of the final satanic triple alliance, when the Sabbath will be the special point of contention. This is the reason why many Adventists will join the ranks of the opposition in the end.

God is now searching for those who will be carried forward by His Spirit in giving the loud cry of the last warning message to depart from the system of sin. This is the moment when "the sins of Babylon will be laid open. The fearful results of enforcing the observances of the church by civil authority, the inroads of spiritualism, the stealthy but rapid progress of the papal power—all will be unmasked."[10]

It is a thrilling thought that we can be participants in bringing the long-standing controversy to a climax. But unless we *are* participants in that final call we shall be lost.

1. *The Great Controversy,* p. 569.
2. *Ibid.*, p. 572.
3. Christopher Wordsworth, *Union With Rome,* quoted in *Seventh-day Adventist Bible Students Source Book,* pp. 90, 91.
4. *The Great Controversy*, pp. 382, 383.
5. *Ibid.*, p. 386
6. *Ibid.*, p. 588.
7. *The Great Controversy*, p. 583.
8. *Christ's Object Lessons*, p. 415.
9. *The Great Controversy*, p. 606.
10. *Ibid.*, p. 606.

"And the third angel followed them, saying with a loud voice, If any man worship the beast and his image, and receive his mark in his forehead, or in his hand, the same shall drink of the wine of the wrath of God, which is poured out without mixture into the cup of his indignation; and he shall be tormented with fire and brimstone in the presence of the holy angels, and in the presence of the Lamb: and the smoke of their torment ascendeth up for ever and ever: and they have no rest day nor night, who worship the beast and his image, and whosoever receiveth the mark of his name."
Revelation 14:9-11.

The Final Test

Nothing in Scripture is comparable to the fearful threat directed at those who receive the mark of the beast. That sin must be terrible which calls forth such a pronouncement of divine wrath! In justice God will not leave humanity in darkness concerning this mark. A warning will be given that men may choose between loyalty and disloyalty. The long-standing controversy, which began in heaven over Satan's freewheeling lawlessness and God's law of love, is about to come to a grand climax. The final test will be over the fourth commandment. Generally speaking, men have no quarrel with the other nine, but there always has been a diabolical animosity directed against the real Lord's day and a determined insistence on forcing allegiance to a man-made substitute, Sunday.

Many may be proclaiming the nearness of the second advent, but their voices are confused with a tangled theology in everything from some secret rapture to what actually is needed in the way of personal preparation for that tremendous event. The urgency of our times requires that Seventh-day Adventists use every skill at their command to present the serious dangers of tampering with the law of God and the need of fully understanding the meaning of the seventh-day Sabbath. Our voices must be unhesitatingly clear in presenting the Sabbath as a sign, not only of Christ as Creator, but also as our Redeemer who is capable of re-creating us in His own image.

Back in the 1960s a chartered 707 approached the Portland International Airport from the east. When the tower cleared the inbound plane for landing, the pilot, unfamiliar with the region, looked down the Columbia River Gorge and spotted a runway just ahead. It happened to be the Troutdale Airport, about ten miles from his destination. Unaware of his error the pilot landed the jet on a runway designed solely for small aircraft. The plane rolled clear to the end of the pavement and fortunately came to a stop just short of a cabbage field. The passengers were obliged to complete their trip by bus to the Portland Airport. But that wasn't all. Before the 707 was light enough for take-off on the short runway all baggage and every passenger seat had to be removed. The pilot may have made an honest mistake, but we may be sure he never repeated the performance!

Many Christians of past ages may have honestly assumed that keeping Sunday was obeying the command to keep the Bible Sabbath. Even today there are true Christians in every persuasion, including Roman Catholics, who conscientiously consider Sunday to be sacred. I can appreciate that.

I grew up in a family that set Sunday aside as a special day. We would never think of washing clothes or hanging them out to dry on the first day of the week. Attending a theater or a ball game on that day was most certainly frowned upon. However, with these restrictions was mixed an assortment of acceptable activities. The inconsistencies never seemed to register with us. Dad thought nothing of mowing the lawn, and we could play ball at home. Sunday was more of a family day than a Sabbath. But when I learned the truth of the Bible Sabbath and its blessings, I never returned to keeping the first day of the week.

No one yet has received the mark of the beast. "But when Sunday observance shall be enforced by law, and the world shall be enlightened concerning the obligation of the true Sabbath, then whoever shall transgress the command of God, to obey a precept which has no higher authority than that of Rome, will thereby honor popery above God. He is paying homage to Rome and to the power which enforces the institution ordained by Rome. He is worshiping the beast and his image. . . . And it is not until the issue is thus plainly set before the people, and they are brought to choose between the commandments of God and the commandments of men, that those who continue in transgression will receive 'the mark of the beast.' "[1]

The role of the United States in this final drama is significant. The prophecy of Revelation 13:15 indicates that this country will have the power to "give life unto the image of the beast." It is not difficult to see how this could happen. The climate for such an event is right. It is easy to collect news releases and factual accounts of religio-political trends that indicate that this prophecy is rapidly unfolding. Reaction from the right wing elements already is driving hard to correct any permissiveness from the left. The "law and order" cry carries with it a tendency toward intolerance and persecution. Those who use the government to enforce their preferences in any religiously-tainted issue will never hesitate to clamor for a return to strict enforcement of the so-called "Lord's day." Increasing natural disasters, revolting crimes, terrorism, world chaos, calamities, and commotions all lend themselves to those whose minds are set on demanding government backing in their efforts to improve society through their particular brand of religion.

Satan well knows how reaction works. The mounting pressures from the forces of evil invariably produce a panic, and the people, like frightened, huddled sheep, will seek protection in any leader who promises deliverance. Although vastly in the minority, Hitler and his Nazi thugs stepped into the chaotic conditions of Germany in 1933. It became no great trick to turn the attention of the people toward a Jewish scapegoat. The repetition of a similar scenario in this country is well within the realm of reality in our time. The mentality of many people is ripe for such a repudiation of the principles upon which this country was founded.

And linked with this great reform movement back to the so-called "Christian Sabbath" will likely be an anti-drug and anti-alcohol theme. It has happened before. Suddenly Adventists who cannot accept Sunday legislation could find themselves branded as enemies of temperance and reform, and suspiciously linked with the lower elements of society.

The devil is an old hand at false accusations. He will use the same tactics he employed when the conflict opened in heaven. There he accused the loyal angels of the very evils which he himself was secretly initiating, all the while loudly proclaiming his concern for maintaining the stability of the divine government.

"So it will be now. While Satan seeks to destroy those who honor God's law, he will cause them to be accused as lawbreakers, as men who are dishonoring God and bringing judgments upon the world."[2]

It takes no great stretch of the imagination to visualize various scenarios in which no person can buy or sell unless he is willing to cooperate with the state in the matter of Sunday observance. Finances will figure fully in the pressure to conform. Receiving the mark of the beast will seem to be the easiest, the most sensible, the most logical thing to do. While this mark is not something visible, it will be known by all heaven.

The Bible says that this mark can be received, either in the forehead or in the hand—either as a matter of misguided conviction or mere convenience. The forehead is the seat of man's will and conscience. It is here where the seal of God is placed. Some, in full knowledge that the Sabbath is God's rest day, will choose to serve a man-made sabbath, all evidence to the contrary notwithstanding. Others, however, will receive the mark in their hand rather than lose their jobs. "I have to support myself and my family," will seem to be a conclusive reason for such individuals.

At the beginning of World War II the world anxiously watched the French and German standoff for eight tense months. This waiting game became known as "The Phony War." Hitler moved his troops threateningly up to the Rhine. The French braced themselves, remembering how the Germans had swept into their country in World War I.

This time, however, they seemed prepared for any assault.

Huddled deep within the bowels of the earth within the famous Maginot Line that ran from the Swiss border to Flanders, they appeared secure against attack. The French even boasted that whoever dared fire the first shot at them would get hurt. Safe in their air-conditioned bunkers, they rested in the knowledge that they had plenty of food, water, ammunition, and even underground garages and airplane hangars leading to surface roads and runways.

But the Germans had no intention of provoking an immediate fight. Once they were in place they simply sent balloons wafting toward the French with neat little propaganda leaflets. "Why are you down in your holes?" the messages read. "We only seek peace." The Germans also played stirring French music over loudspeakers and sent more messages both orally and by leaflet. Over and over the same messages came, with an incessant softening technique, and often with added suggestions designed to reach the heart of every French soldier. Some of these said: "While you are waiting below ground your British supporters are running off with your wives and sweethearts." Day after day more music and messages came. The French, who were already less than enthusiastic about fighting a war, became ripe for exploitation. Morale within the ranks slipped lower and lower.

Suddenly on May 10, 1940, all the phoniness of "The Phony War" evaporated as the Nazi war machine roared forward in a smashing end run through Belgium, Luxemburg, and the Ardennes forest. The German juggernaut rolled on until France collapsed and was forced on June 22 to sign a most humiliating surrender document—ironically in the same railroad car that had been used by the Allies when the Germans capitulated at the end of World War I. And what happened to the vaunted Maginot Line? All those heavy artillery pieces remained intact. Not a shot had been fired!

Today Satan is using the mass media for a softening up and disarming technique designed to create a climate in which eternal values are exchanged for human devisings. The enemy knows full well the principle that by beholding we become changed. Books, magazines, newspapers, radio, TV, and movies have blanketed the earth like a London fog, advocating the sentiment that anything goes. Comedians, comics books, and commentators follow the suggestion of the master mind of evil in destroying everything decent, sacred, and pure. From marriage to morals, it is always the same theme—every man is a law unto himself.

One basic essential common to all successful propaganda is the principle of repeating a lie so often that in the end it is accepted as truth. When men accept by repetition the enemy's concept that anything related to the law of God is legalistic and man can cheat his way through any race, it will be no great trick to manipulate the mind into nodding approval of a Sunday law. "The line of distinction between professed Christians and the ungodly is now hardly distinguishable. Church members love what the world loves and are ready to join with them, and Satan determines to unite them in one body and thus strengthen his cause by sweeping all into the ranks of spiritualism. . . . Papists, protestants, and worldlings will alike accept the form of godliness without the power, and they will see in this union a grand movement for the conversion of the world and the ushering in of the long-expected millennium."[3]

The process of shaping minds to accept the mark of the beast should be considered a life-and-death matter. Everything is now at stake. Satan is doing his utmost to divert people from preparing for the final test over the law of God. Besides tapping into every fragment of carnality possible, he uses the standard format of keeping the nations embroiled in wars and stirring up natural disasters. Having studied both the inner workings of nature and the psychology of depraved minds, he has honed the techniques of destruction to a fine point. Even political corruption has a place in his diversionary scheme. Such corruption in high government places destroys the love of justice and regard for truth, and when the popular demand for Sunday legislation picks up steam, politicians will easily yield rather than lose votes. But, whatever the avenue, we must be alert to what the enemy is up to in his final showdown effort on this planet.

The way you value the Sabbath today will determine the side on which you will stand in the conflict tomorrow. If God's rest day means no more than attending church, enjoying a big meal, and then discussing everything from politics to bargain-price discoveries, then when the pressure mounts to keep Sunday, the Sabbath will seem unimportant. On the other hand, if the Lord's Sabbath is to us such a blessing that it signifies a genuine chance to have closer fellowship with Him in every aspect of the word, from associations to finding a peace in His created works, then that day will become a day worth going to the wall for.

Once, when I stepped into an Adventist servicemen's center on Sabbath, a couple of the men were intensely consumed in a game of what might be called "vegetarian billiards." The chaplain, distinctly embarrassed, went over and whispered to them with a frown, "Put the game away, men." They obeyed, but I thought to myself, "Do we have to be watched?" God is seeking those who will show Him affection and reverence. The Sabbath is always a high day for such an experience with Him. It is the Holy Spirit who will lead all who are willing into such a relationship. Men cannot keep the Sabbath holy unless they are made holy through His power. "The sanctification of the Spirit signalizes the difference between those who have the seal of God and those who keep a spurious rest day."[4]

The touch of God's Spirit will enable the faithful to do that which could not have been done before, and this will give them a power not witnessed since apostolic times. One of the major effects of this outpouring of the Spirit will be to stir up those who despise Adventists. "The power attending the message will only madden those who oppose it."[5] Suddenly every news media known will blazon the issues that at last have come into focus. ABC, CBS, and NBC will carry it live without costing Seventh-day Adventists a cent. Prior to this we have spent millions trying to reach people; now the world will really be listening.

"As the question of enforcing Sunday observance is widely agitated, the event so long doubted and disbelieved is seen to be approaching, and the third [angel's] message will produce an effect which it could not have had before."[6] Adventists will be thrust forward onto center stage, where a lot of questions will be asked.

Opponents will seek to use the old courtroom ploy of diverting attention to other matters in guilt by association. Past denominational mistakes will be flaunted as part of Satan's smear technique, but the truth of God's message must be maintained regardless of any diversionary tactics. Since the Sabbath is the great test of loyalty, that is the focal point toward which attention must be directed. And the maintenance of that focus will most certainly enable the honest seekers of truth to find it.

A side effect of all this will be the sifting that takes place within the ranks of the Adventist Church itself. "As the storm approaches, a large class who have professed faith in the third angel's message, but who have not been sanctified through obedience to the truth, abandon their position, and join the ranks of the opposition. By uniting with the world and partaking of its spirit, they have come to view matters in nearly the same light; and when the test is brought, they are prepared to choose the easy, popular side."[7]

We most certainly have a heaven to win and a hell to shun. For those who will be alive upon this earth when Jesus comes there is either the thrill of being translated or the horror of enduring the seven last plagues plus the final separation that takes place at the close of the millennium.

While the words of the book of Revelation are generally highly symbolic, its description of the reward of saint and sinner is very real. Eternal life is reserved for the obedient. Now is our day to prepare. "If the believers in the truth are not sustained by their faith in these comparatively peaceful times, what will uphold them when the grand test comes and the decree goes forth against all those who will not worship

the image of the beast and receive his mark in their fore-
heads or in their hands?"[8] The words of that ancient
prophet Amos, when he thundered at those smug worship-
ers at Bethel who had settled into a religious complacency,
seem singularly appropriate now—"Prepare to meet thy
God, O Israel!" Amos 4:12.

1. *The Great Controversy*, p. 449.
2. *Ibid.*, p. 591.
3. *Ibid.*, pp. 588, 589.
4. Ellen G. White Comments, *SDA Bible Commentary*, vol. 7, p. 980.
5. *The Great Controversy*, p. 607.
6. *Ibid.*, p. 606.
7. *Ibid.*, p. 608.
8. *Testimonies*, vol. 4, p. 251.

"Here is the patience of the saints." Revelation 14:12:

The Patience of the Saints

During the early thirties when the great depression had settled into every crack and cranny of society like so much fine dust, it became increasingly difficult for some people to own respectable-looking dress clothes. Henry was a poor preacher who knew that his threadbare suit wouldn't last much longer, so he scrimped and saved for months prior to camp meeting. Finally he managed to save thirty-five dollars, a lot of money in those days, to purchase a good quality suit.

In the midst of camp pitch the conference president held a workers' meeting in which he made an eloquent plea for sacrificial giving. "After all," the president explained, "we can't expect our people to give unless we ourselves have shown the way."

As the plate was passed Henry was so deeply moved that he reached into his pocket and put in the entire thirty-five dollars he had saved. Somehow he would make do with his old suit.

When opening night of camp meeting arrived, the conference president asked that the entire ministerial force appear on the platform with him so the congregation could see all the preachers. Henry lined up outside the main tent with his colleagues, but when the conference president spied his old, worn suit he went over and whispered, "I think it best you not go up on the platform tonight. Your suit really isn't very representative."

Henry felt the heat rise in his face. Quickly stepping aside, he hurried to his tent and dropped to his knees. "Oh, God," he cried, "that hurt so much!"

His good wife found him later and, after learning what had happened, put her arm around his shoulders and said quietly, "Well, Henry, that certainly was an insensitive blow. But maybe out of this experience you can develop more of the patience of the saints."

Maybe someone should have taken that conference president aside and explained the situation in terms he could understand, but the point is that Henry did gain some valuable insights into that rare virtue called patience.

One of the outstanding identifying marks of the saints of God is their patience. As Seventh-day Adventists we are in dire need of understanding this important feature of our faith. We may be sustained in our positions by an overwhelming amount of solid scriptural authority, but we most certainly are lacking in some of those practical biblical virtues. And one of the most glaring is this matter of patience. Through the years I have become painfully aware of this lack which needs to be corrected before Jesus can come and claim us as His own.

Shortly after my wife and I were married we started attending prayer meeting at Walla Walla College. One evening we took a shortcut behind the music conservatory. It had rained all day and the ground was oozing with soft, wet mud. Coming to a small embankment about six feet high, I quickly handed my Bible to my wife and scrambled up, intending to help her up the slippery slope. As she reached for my hand, she accidentally dropped my Bible in the mud. I exploded with a volley of select, impatient words, which included *stupid, clumsy, awkward,* and other choice synonyms. To her credit, my wife never replied in kind, not then nor in the intervening years. She was truly sorry, and we went on to prayer meeting where I sat glumly, stewing over the incident.

I can't remember one thing about that prayer meeting, but I most certainly recall what happened the next day when I hastily grabbed my Bible and headed for class. Seated among the other students I flipped through the pages to find any evidence of the night before. The mud had all been cleaned away, and the page where it had torn was neatly repaired. I never could tape anything perfectly, but my dear wife had carefully mended the damaged page. Then I did a double take. The repaired spot was Ephesians 5:25: "Husbands, love your wives, even as Christ also loved the church, and gave himself for it." Seldom have I received a more appropriate rebuke!

Later when the children arrived and life became far more involved, father would often find himself tremendously tense the moment the noise factor in the home rose. At those junctures my wife would quietly quote, "Here is the patience of the saints." And when our girls were older and their father would be making those impatient noises of frustration over some trivial matter, they would huddle in the corner and sing in response, "With Jesus in the family, happy, happy home!" What lessons in patience they all taught me!

Most of us, of course, have a flat side. With many impatience seems to predominate. The highway, for instance, has a tendency to bring out latent forces of self-expression—mutterings about women drivers, or men whose mothers taught them to drive, is common. In my case, a lost article which I just had in my hand, toilets that won't flush, or striking my anatomy on some solid object can bring out as much impatience as any highway.

I wonder if we always realize that God permits these things that try our patience to develop patience in us. I remember I once decided to pray specifically about my problem with impatience. I selected a secluded spot in the woods and knelt down to discuss the matter with God. When I arose from prayer, I bumped my head squarely on an overhanging branch! But this time, instead of becoming angry and impatient, I burst out laughing. Somehow the whole irony of the situation touched my humorous side, and I ended up thanking God for His unique manner of answering my prayer.

Any display of impatience is an indication that self is still very much alive. This takes us back to Revelation 14:7: "Give glory to him." The patience of the saints is not possible without a death to self. Ellen White so pointedly wrote this counsel to a very impatient man: "Those who are dead to self will not feel so readily and will not be prepared to resist everything which may irritate. Dead men cannot feel. You are not dead. If you were, and your life were hid in Christ, a thousand things which you now notice, and which afflict you, would be passed by as unworthy of notice; you would then be grasping the eternal and would be above the petty trials of this life."[1]

A better translation of Revelation 14:12 might actually read, "Here is the steadfast endurance of the saints." Remember that it is in the context of the fearful struggle with the threefold power of spiritualism, apostate Protestantism and the papacy that this appears. Every attempt will be made to force those who maintain their allegiance to God to yield. But neither bribery, nor boycott, nor threat of death can alter the saints' hold on God. Even under such supreme pressure they remain faithful, and their steadfast endurance calls forth heaven's commendation.

When Jesus spoke of persecution and how men would hate God's people, He punctuated the need for endurance. "He that shall endure unto the end, the same shall be saved," He said. Matthew 24:13. And again, "In your patience possess ye your souls." Luke 21:19. Endurance and patience are connected in Scripture with the joy of those who are one with the Lord. Job is singled out as an outstanding example. "Behold, we count them happy which endure." James 5:11. Most certainly Job was not joyful during his affliction, but a happy ending followed his suffering hours, when he prayed for his "comforters" and willingly resigned his fate into the hands of his Maker. Without fussing or fuming, which could only aggravate the situation,

Job let go and let God handle his case. And in that he left us a worthy example of persevering patience under extreme stress.

When the unseen forces of evil combine with the threefold religious, earthly powers to throw everything in their diabolical arsenal at God's true people, we shall need the kind of firm faith that is seldom witnessed. "The season of distress and anguish before us will require a faith that can endure weariness, delay, and hunger—a faith that will not fail, though severely tried. . . . How few have ever had their souls drawn out after God with intensity of desire until every power is on the stretch. When waves of despair which no language can express sweep over the suppliant, how few cling with unyielding faith to the promises of God."[2] But the problem is that we live in a climate of instant satisfaction. Society has been conditioned to demand answers NOW—yesterday, if possible! Punch a button or pop a pill and all is supposed to be well. Delay is irksome. But God in His infinite wisdom has left us lessons in nature that teach us patience.

The sun will set, the tide will come in, the bulb will bloom, and the seed will sprout *in its season*. We cannot hurry sundown, hasten the tide, or do much about bulbs or seeds except as we cooperate with nature in her steady course. If understood correctly, so much of nature holds immeasurably valuable lessons of resigned calmness for coping with life itself and for preparing for future events when everything will be on the line. Those lessons learned today will demonstrate the patience of the saints tomorrow.

Not in freedom from trials, but in the midst of rebuffs and opposition is Christian character developed. Exposure to such stressful situations may not seem pleasant, but it leads the follower of Jesus to seek Him who stands ready as a mighty Helper in time of need. If we are ever going to develop the patience of the saints we must have obstacle courses to strengthen our spiritual endurance.

I used to run obstacle courses, and I hated them at the time. The army training program sent raw recruits with full field packs up and down rope ladders, under and over logs, and hand over hand on swinging ropes until it seemed that every bone and muscle ached with the exertion. Crawling on my belly the length of a football field with sweat pouring down my face in the hot Texas sun could never be classified as fun. I despised the training and wrote home to express my dislike, seeking sympathy from my parents. I wrote even more when the military forced me to crawl into live machine gun fire just eighteen inches above ground level. And then to have some officer smugly standing in a nearby tower pulling levers to activate powder charges strategically placed in barbed-wire-laced holes all over the infiltration course simulating shell bursts squeezed more tearful letters from me. Dad and Mom would understand. Maybe they could write their congressman about all the awful things the army was doing to their boy. But when I landed on Okinawa at the tail end of the battle, I was more than glad for all the training. It paid off. And it will pay off in the spiritual life as well.

"Had there been nothing in the world to work at cross purposes with us, patience, forebearance, gentleness, meekness, and longsuffering would not have been called into action. The more these graces are exercised, the more will they be increased and strengthened."[3]

Moses had to learn patience this way. It was in God's providence that he herded sheep for so many years. We can only imagine his impatient frustration at first at these "dumb creatures." He probably shouted and threw rocks at the sheep during his early training. After all, he had been commander of armies in Egypt and expected immediate obedience. But sheep don't obey very well. They can act awfully stupid, scattering in every direction at the least hint of danger. So Moses learned. He received an education which no amount of scholarly research, study, or knowledge could give. In the process he became forgetful of self and interested in the welfare of the flock under his charge. Thus he finally fitted himself to become the great leader of Israel, one of the most exalted roles ever committed to a mortal.

God has provided a few simple measures to assist us in daily development of our patience. Silence is one of them. When impatient words come flying at us, this is the time to be silent. Responding in kind only acts as a whip, lashing a temper already out of control into wild fury. But anger met with silence quickly dies away. And while your tongue is bridled, pray. When you are on the verge of yielding to impatience and losing self-control in a volley of caustic, harsh words, send up a prayer that the Holy Spirit will take away the bitterness and wrath by filling your mind with the calmness of God that truly represents the Saviour.

Sometimes even singing or whistling can be effective. This is one of the methods Jesus used. "Sorely as he was tried on the point of hasty and angry speech, he never once sinned with his lips. With patient calmness he met the sneers, the taunts, and the ridicule of his fellow workers at the carpenter's bench. Instead of retorting angrily, he would begin to sing one of David's beautiful psalms; and his companions, before realizing what they were doing, would unite with him in the hymn. What a transformation would be wrought in this world if men and women to-day would follow Christ's example in the use of words!"[4]

Once in the women's ward of a state penitentiary the inmates broke into a violent riot, screaming, tearing, clawing, and cursing. At the height of the melee, someone began to sing. Her voice rose steadily above the din, until all could hear that old familiar gospel song, "Yield not to temptation, for yielding is sin." The singing continued as if the singer were oblivious to the surrounding anger. Slowly but steadily a transformation took place. The noise subsided as one by one the inmates settled down and returned peacefully to their cells.

It is in the small skirmishes of life that we gain courage for the big battles ahead. Every day can have its little unsung victories that prepare us for the test that is coming. If we gain these victories, we shall not have to make excuses and say, "I was off my guard; I didn't mean what I said." Heaven doesn't treat impatience lightly. God's Word teaches us that small losses and defeats not overcome can eventually crush us. When something comes your way to test patience, remember that it is an opportunity to prepare yourself for the coming crisis. Of those who learn this lesson, God says, "Here is the patience of the saints!"

1. *Testimonies,* vol. 2, p. 425.
2. *The Great Controversy,* p. 621.
3. Ellen G. White, *Welfare Minstry,* p. 306.
4. Ellen G. White, *Review and Herald,* May 26, 1904.

"Here are they that keep the commandments of God, and the faith of Jesus." Revelation 14:12.

With Our Pilot on Board

During a friendly discussion with a Mormon leader one evening I was suddenly taken aback when this church official exclaimed, "Latter Day Saints have a Bible text for proof they are the true church!"

"What's that?" I asked.

"Revelation 12:17."

"Well, now, that's interesting," I remarked. "Seventh-day Adventists lay claim to that text too."

"Oh, but we have the spirit of prophecy!" he countered.

I well understood his reference to Revelation 19:10, but quickly slipped him a bit of information he probably had not noticed before. "But we have the spirit of prophecy too!" I exclaimed.

His eyebrows arched. "You do?"

"Yes. Would you like to read what our prophet had to say about the last days?"

He nodded weakly, his mouth still agape with surprise. I hurried inside my house and grabbed a copy of *The Great Controversy*. When I returned he was still standing there in the twilight with that same stunned expression on his face. As I handed him the gift edition he thanked me politely, then quickly terminated the conversation and departed for parts unknown. I never heard from him again.

But I had some questions. It is one thing to recognize the significance of the spirit of prophecy as an earmark of the remnant church, but quite another to understand the function of that gift which never goes counter to the revealed teachings of Scripture. Considering his church's concept of the spirit of prophecy, which does not build solidly on past revelations of Jesus Christ in Scripture, I wondered how he could make such a claim.

But this isn't all. What about commandment keeping? I knew that his church did not observe the Bible Sabbath and wondered why they did not, if they were supposed to be an extension of that long line of believers down through the ages who have stood so valiantly for the law of God.

But Seventh-day Adventists should have no qualms about laying claim to Revelation 12:17. While we may not have grasped the full significance of the message we are to bear about God's character, either collectively or individually, or even lived up to all revealed light, we can unflinchingly maintain our position as the remnant, both biblically and historically. No other people come close to fitting the identifying description of God's last representatives who are commissioned to call people out of the darkness of superstition and tradition into God's marvelous light.

So many shots have been fired at legalism that many have become a bit gun shy in presenting the truths of God's law. But true commandment keeping and legalism are never compatible. We should never hesitate to raise our voices with the psalmist in declaring, "Open thou mine eyes, that I may behold wondrous things out of thy law." Psalm 119:18. The saints of God will keep those commandments both inwardly and outwardly because of His transforming power of love. Obedience must never be understood to be an obligation or some performance record for gaining merit. Rather, it is a natural outworking of Christ's life in us by the operation of the Spirit on the heart—God working in us willing and doing His good pleasure. See Philippians 2:13.

When God spoke that first commandment telling us not to have any gods before Him, those who love Him supremely respond by saying, "I want nothing in my life that will lessen my love for God nor retain anything that will interfere with the worship due Him."

While the first commandment concerns itself with our concept of God, the second deals with the external acts of worship. "Little children, keep yourselves from idols" (1 John 5:21), was written by John, not to image-worshiping heathen, but to Christians. And the true follower of Christ will want to have no part of image making or idol worship, either in its grosser forms or its more open manifestations as expressed, for instance, by following the goddess of fashion or lusting after the opposite sex.

Not taking God's name in vain is more than a simple prohibition against false oaths and common swearing. It encompasses meaningless repetition of His sacred name or the careless use of His name, as well as borderline expressions that dishonor Deity. Words such as *gee* for Jesus lower that precious name. Today it is common practice to insert the word *God* into all types of conversation, but the true Christian shudders at such thoughtless usage and is saddened by the cheapening of the One he loves.

The true Sabbath keeper will find this day an exciting time slot to worship God for His creative genius, not only as a memorial of the world's creation, but of His power to recreate *us* in His own image through Jesus. All the activities, the conversation and usage of these sacred hours, will reflect the importance of this special weekly appointment with Him.

The fifth commandment not only opens to believers opportunities to show respect to parents, "but also to give them love and tenderness, to lighten their cares, to guard their reputation, and to succor and comfort them in old age."[1] Those who are willing to search deeper into the law know that it also enjoins respect for ministers and all those to whom God has delegated authority.

"Thou shalt not kill" certainly means more than engaging in some violent act of murder. It reaches down to the very intents of the heart in those ugly feelings of hatred. When the tongue lashes out in character assassination or a person practices self-indulgence or neglects to help the needy and suffering, this commandment is violated. Those who reflect the image of Jesus will be above hateful or self-centered thoughts and actions.

The seventh commandment touches not only outward acts of impurity, but sensual thoughts, desires, and practices that stimulate them. Those who realize the purity of God will seek to bring every thought and emotion into captivity to Christ who alone can conquer the clamorings of the flesh.

In an age when every attempt is made to take advantage of someone else's ignorance, weakness, or misfortune, the eighth commandment is especially applicable. The true Christian will see in this commandment an opportunity to demonstrate love in every transaction of life and will maintain a strict integrity in all affairs.

Bearing false witness could be classified as "the forgotten commandment." While the third safeguards the name of God, the ninth protects the reputation of men. Any attempt to deceive our neighbor is included, and this means body language as well as spoken words. A glance of the eye, a shrug of the shoulders, or a tongue-in-cheek remark can overstate the facts or convey an erroneous impression. Even slanting the facts to mislead is falsehood. Any effort to injure someone's reputation by evil surmising, slander, or gossip means transgression. Long ago the Bible knew about this kind of unspoken language, when it said of "the wicked man . . .winketh with his eyes, he speaketh with his feet, he teacheth with his fingers." Proverbs 6:12, 13.

"Even the intentional suppression of truth, by which injury may result to others, is a violation of the ninth commandment."[2] Silence isn't always golden; sometimes it's just plain yellow! The true commandment keeper will ever be sensitive to the touch of the Holy Spirit in dealing with others.

The tenth commandment strikes directly at the nerve center of selfish desire where all sinful acts originate. Whether idolatry, hypocrisy, Sabbath breaking, dishonoring parents, murder, adultery, stealing, lying, or bearing false witness, they can all be traced to covetousness. This commandment is therefore a summary of all ten. Covetousness was the root trouble when the great controversy began. True love to God and man is willing to allow the penetrating probing of the Holy Spirit to examine every recess of the heart that it may always be free from selfish desire.

Satan has claimed from the beginning that the law of God could not be kept. He is still harping on this theme—with enough choruses from his human agents to make it sound plausible! But God in His great gift of Jesus made such ample provision that we need never be brought into a position where yielding to evil becomes a necessity. We need never be defeated by the enemy, no matter how severe the temptation to transgress.

When Jesus said, "If ye love me, keep my commandments" (John 14:15) He underscored the truth concerning heart religion. Love and obedience are inseparable. When Jesus abides in the heart, the very inflection of the voice in reading the law shifts to a positive note. Every "thou shalt not" solicits a "why?" and quickly comes the answer, "Because I love You, Lord, and I love my fellowman. I do not wish to do anything that would cause separation, destruction, or hurt to anyone."

When understood in this way, each of the Ten Commandments leaps from the decalog with positive appeal because of that love which was so beautifully demonstrated in the life of Christ. With Him obedience to the Ten Commandments was never a checklist religion. His obedience came from the heart—"I delight to do thy will, O my God: yea, thy law is within my heart." Psalm 40:8. We are assured that, "if we consent, He will so identify Himself with our thoughts and aims, so blend our hearts and minds into conformity to His will, that when obeying Him we shall be but carrying out our own impulses. The will, refined and sanctified, will find its highest delight in doing His service. When we know God as it is our privilege to know Him, our life will be a life of continual obedience. Through an appreciation of the character of Christ, through communion with God, sin will become hateful to us."[3]

Knowing God is the key! John 17:3 has special significance to us: "This is life eternal, that they might know thee the only true God, and Jesus Christ, whom thou hast sent." It is not knowing *about* Him, but *knowing* Him personally that produces hatred of sin. That knowledge reaches down to the thoughts, the feelings, and the very purposes of life. It results in more than just outward actions because it elevates us into harmony with God's will. Spontaneous obedience out of love becomes a driving force in the life and captivates the entire being.

A large neon sign atop a Hollywood night club caught my attention as it flashed, "Welcome Sinner." The words often used to call sinners to Christ obviously were intended to convey another meaning. Such cynical advertising is typical of the efforts of Satan's agents to play up sensual pleasures while at the same time defiantly magnifying the lost condition of those whose evil propensities are honed to prostituting and indulging their carnal desires. Somehow worldlings feel more comfortable when others are headed on the downward path with them. But to the person who knows God as a friend, such glittering allurement is wasted. The real Christian has discovered something better, and all efforts of the enemy's forces find no responsive chord. How can there be any response when the knowledge of God opens the mind to the horrible enormity of sin and the high cost of redemption? When we know God, our understanding of His hatred of sin and all its ramifications will be more complete. We begin to think His thoughts.

While Jesus is still in the heavenly sanctuary, we should seek to become so full of the knowledge of God that no room is left for Satan's intrusions. That is how it was with Jesus. When the enemy came to the Son of God he could find nothing that would cause Jesus to yield to his temptations. When he comes to us he often finds some point where he can gain a foothold, some cherished desire whereby his temptations assert their power. We are either hankering after the pleasures of the world, ground down with the cares of this life, stewing about the faults of others, rehearsing our past mistakes and imperfections, or worrying about whether or not we will be saved. The devil does not care which card we pick, so long as our attention is shifted enough to prevent a union and communion with the Saviour.

That is why we urgently need to seek the aid of the Holy Spirit when studying the Scriptures or contemplating lessons from nature. We can never really know God without His aid. Apart from God's Spirit, the mind warped by outside influences and internal clamorings will reach erroneous conclusions about God's character, and our lives will never be transformed by His power.

When Jesus told His disciples "The prince of this world cometh, and hath nothing in me" (John 14:30), He left us a most encouraging word. "He had kept His Father's commandments, and there was no sin in Him that Satan could use to his advantage. *This is the condition in which those must be found who shall stand in the time of trouble*."[4] For those whose focus may be on self this may not sound so encouraging, but in reality it is most cheering because "our precious Saviour invites us to join ourselves to Him, to unite our weakness to His strength, our ignorance to His wisdom, our unworthiness to His merits."[5] In knowing our Heavenly Father and His longing to save us, and in knowing His Son who showed us the Father in action, we should never hesitate to approach the last moment of this earth's history with complete trust in Him.

The last community of saints not only have an understanding of true love in keeping the commandments, but they also have the "faith of Jesus." Intellectually and spiritually they have settled into the truth about God.

The term "faith of Jesus" may also be understood as "faith in Jesus."[6] Ultimately both concepts reach the same type of trust. It is possible through His power to have the same kind of faith that Jesus possessed. It is also possible to have such faith in Jesus that the life reflects His image fully. It is especially important to grasp this faith factor as we approach the final crisis.

We are now entering that dangerous point in history when

we need our Pilot on board. Such an idea may conjure up a scene of Jesus taking the wheel and guiding us through the treacherous waters to the "haven of rest." Artists have contributed to this misconception, and so has that old gospel song, "Jesus, Saviour, Pilot Me." But this is an inaccurate picture when it comes to bar pilots.

Harbor pilots come aboard to guide ships into harbors, river pilots navigate ships down the great water courses. But it is the work of bar pilots to negotiate the dangerous bars where the river and the sea meet, and the manner in which they operate is important to our understanding of "crossing the bar" at the end of time.

In all the years of my work as free-lance writer and photographer, nothing taught me a greater lesson in total trust than the assignment to ride with the Columbia River bar pilots.

Most great rivers, such as the Amazon, Congo, Ganges, or the Mississippi, soften their approaches to the sea with deltas. But not the Columbia! It has the worst river bar in the world! So notorious has it become through the years that the coastal waters near the bar are known as the Pacific Graveyard. Here many ships have gone aground trying to cross the bar without a pilot. After a 1400-mile torturous rush down from the Canadian ice field, the river slams into the Pacific at the rate of a million cubic feet of water per second. The commotion of the shifting sand and silt wreaks havoc with shipping. Before a bridge was built miles down river near Astoria, even the old ferryboats with their shallow draft used to get hung up. The widest part of the Columbia bar is 3,000 yards across, and at ebb tide, with the water moving out to sea at 15 to 24 knots, it is an awesome spectacle. Even on calm days great waves known as "grandpappies" as much as forty feet high come roaring and hissing at eye level as viewed from the bridge of the bigger ships.

The "middle ground" is the most dangerous. With additional strength of a gale it becomes positively frightful. But when the wind reaches hurricane force—80 to 90 miles an hour or more as it roars out of the southwest—nothing in all nature compares with its fury. No wonder all shipping ceases during such storms!

When I did the photo feature previously referred to, there were not more than a dozen registered pilots who guided ships in and out over the Columbia bar. These men represented the cream of skippers. Most had sailed the great oceans of the world for many years and were considered to be the epitome of success as the masters of ships. They had taken up residence at Astoria, Oregon, where they could be home every evening and still accept the challenge and responsibility for guiding the great ships safely into port.

The pilot boat, a converted mine sweeper from World War II, would leave Astoria in the morning with a party of pilots aboard and wait several miles out at sea for the ships to approach the bar. When a ship came up over the horizon the pilot would have a sailor row him in a dingy to the incoming ship. He would then climb the rope ladder dropped from the ship's side and immediately take up his duties as bar pilot in the wheelhouse.

I wanted to get pictures of an ebb tide crossing and had to wait nearly all day while wallowing in the rolling sea aboard the pilot boat before a ship hove in sight. Finally a huge tanker arrived late in the afternoon. After being rowed to its side I scrambled up the rope ladder ahead of the pilot.

Once on board I witnessed something I shall never forget. The pilot *never touched* the wheel. He stood directly behind the helmsman and gave orders in a quiet voice.

"Left 85," came the command.

Back came the helmsman's confirmation, "Left 85," as he turned the great ship 85 degrees to port.

"Right 15."

"Right 15." Following the pilot's instructions implicitly, the helmsman turned the ship 15 degrees to starboard.

Down the dangerous channel we zigzagged. The pilot is so sensitive to trouble that he can, as they say, tell when the ship is "smelling bottom." When the ship's keel comes close to scraping the pilot orders an evasive movement. It was exciting to observe the pilot and the helmsman working in tandem, one giving the orders, the other obeying without question. That great ship arrived safely in Astoria, where the ship's pilot and I disembarked safely, all because of trust in and obedience to the bar pilot.

My mind pictured Jesus standing behind me, gently instructing me to turn to the left or right. I must never assume to be master of my own ship and turn where I feel like turning. I cannot afford to ignore His orders. With so much wind and sand and shifting silt, and the waters crashing around me, I must obey implicitly or make shipwreck of my life. But by trusting my Pilot, I can safely reach heaven's port safely and finally have the privilege of turning around and seeing my Pilot face to face, when I have crossed the bar.

---

1. Ellen G. White, *Sons and Daughters of God*, p. 60.
2. *Patriarchs and Prophets*, p. 309.
3. *The Desire of Ages*, p. 668.
4. *The Great Controversy*, p. 623, emphasis supplied.
5. *Ibid*.
6. See *SDA Bible Commentary*, vol. 7, p. 833.